W9-CBV-926

Praise for Dixie Browning:

"There is no one writing romance today
who touches the heart and tickles the ribs like
Dixie Browning. The people in her books are as
warm and real as a sunbeam and just as lovely."
—*New York Times* bestselling author Nora Roberts

"Dixie Browning has given the romance industry
years of love and laughter in her wonderful books."
—*New York Times* bestselling author Linda Howard

"Each of Dixie's books is a keeper guaranteed
to warm the heart and delight the senses."
—*New York Times* bestselling author
Jayne Ann Krentz

"A true pioneer in romantic fiction, the delightful
Dixie Browning is a reader's most precious treasure,
a constant source of outstanding entertainment."
—*Romantic Times*

"Dixie's books never disappoint—
they always lift your spirit!"
—*USA TODAY* bestselling author Mary Lynn Baxter

BECKETT'S FORTUNE

Where the price of family and honor is love...

**Don't miss the continuation of this exciting
new series from Silhouette Desire and
Harlequin Historicals:**

**BECKETT'S BIRTHRIGHT
HARLEQUIN HISTORICALS 11/02**

**BECKETT'S CONVENIENT BRIDE
SILHOUETTE DESIRE 1/03**

Dear Reader,

Dog days of summer got you down? Chill out and relax with six brand-new love stories from Silhouette Desire!

August's MAN OF THE MONTH is the first book in the exciting family-based saga BECKETT'S FORTUNE by Dixie Browning. *Beckett's Cinderella* features a hero honor-bound to repay a generations-old debt and a poor-but-proud heroine leery of love and money she can't believe is offered unconditionally. *His E-Mail Order Wife* by Kristi Gold, in which matchmaking relatives use the Internet to find a high-powered exec a bride, is the latest title in the powerful DYNASTIES: THE CONNELLYS series.

A daughter seeking revenge discovers love instead in *Falling for the Enemy* by Shawna Delacorte. Then, in *Millionaire Cop & Mom-To-Be* by Charlotte Hughes, a jilted, pregnant bride is rescued by her childhood sweetheart.

Passion flares between a family-minded rancher and a marriage-shy divorcée in Kathie DeNosky's *Cowboy Boss*. And a pretend marriage leads to undeniable passion in *Desperado Dad* by Linda Conrad.

So find some shade, grab a cold one…and read all six passionate, powerful and provocative new love stories from Silhouette Desire this month.

Enjoy!

Joan Marlow Golan

Joan Marlow Golan
Senior Editor, Silhouette Desire

Please address questions and book requests to:
Silhouette Reader Service
U.S.: 3010 Walden Ave., P.O. Box 1325, Buffalo, NY 14269
Canadian: P.O. Box 609, Fort Erie, Ont. L2A 5X3

Beckett's
Cinderella
DIXIE BROWNING

Published by Silhouette Books

America's Publisher of Contemporary Romance

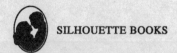

SILHOUETTE BOOKS

ISBN 0-373-76453-7

BECKETT'S CINDERELLA

Copyright © 2002 by Dixie Browning

This edition published by arrangement with Harlequin Books S.A.

® and TM are trademarks of Harlequin Books S.A., used under license. Trademarks indicated with ® are registered in the United States Patent and Trademark Office, the Canadian Trade Marks Office and in other countries.

Visit Silhouette at www.eHarlequin.com

Printed in U.S.A.

DIXIE BROWNING

is an award-winning painter and writer, mother and grandmother. Her father was a big-league baseball player, her grandfather a sea captain. In addition to her nearly eighty contemporary romances, Dixie and her sister, Mary Williams, have written more than a dozen historical romances under the name Bronwyn Williams. Contact Dixie at www.dixiebrowning.com, or at P.O. Box 1389, Buxton, NC 27920.

To the wonderful and caring staff
at Britthaven Nursing Home in Kitty Hawk, N.C.
You're the best!

One

Just before his descent into Norfolk International Airport, Lancelot Beckett opened his briefcase, took out a thin sheaf of paper and scanned a genealogical chart. In the beginning, all they'd had to go on was a name, an approximate birthplace and a rough time line. Now, after God knows how many generations, the job was finally going to get done.

"What the hell do I know about tracking down the descendents of an Oklahoma cowboy born roughly a hundred and fifty years ago?" he'd demanded the last time he'd stopped by his cousin Carson's restored shotgun-style house outside Charleston. "When it comes to tracking down pirates, I'm your man, but cowboys? Come on, Car, give me a break."

"Hey, if you can't handle it, I'll take over once

I'm out of this." Carson, a police detective, was pretty well immobilized for the time being in a fiberglass cast. Now and then, even the Beckett luck ran out. About two months earlier, his had. "Looks like something you can do on your way home anyhow, so it's not like you'd have to detour too far off the beaten track."

"You know where I was when Mom tracked me down? I was in Dublin, for crying out loud," Beckett had explained. They were both Becketts, but Lancelot had laid down the law regarding his name when he was eleven. Since then, he'd been called by his last name. Occasionally, tongue-in-cheek, he was referred to as "The Beckett."

"I had to cancel a couple of appointments in London, not to mention a date. Besides, I'm not headed home anytime soon."

What was the point? Officially, home was a two-room office with second-floor living quarters in Wilmington, Delaware. It served well enough as a mailing address and a place to put his feet up for a few days when he happened to be back in the States.

As it turned out, the place where the Chandler woman was thought to be hiding out was roughly halfway between Wilmington and his parents' home in Charleston.

Hiding out was probably the wrong term; relocated might be closer. Whatever her reasons for being in North Carolina instead of Texas, she'd been hard as the devil to track down. It had taken the combined efforts of Carson's police computers, a few unofficial sources and a certified genealogist to locate the woman.

And with all that, it had been a random sighting— something totally off-the-wall—that had finally pinned her down. Grant's Produce and Free Ice Water, located on a peninsula between the North River and the Currituck Sound, somewhere near a place named Bertha, North Carolina. Hell, they didn't even have a street address for her, just a sign along the highway.

Beckett tried to deal with his impatience. He was used to being on the move while his partner stayed in the office handling the paperwork, but this particular job had to do with family matters. It couldn't be delegated. The buck had been passed as far as it would go.

He'd allowed himself a couple of hours after leaving the airport to find the place and another half hour to wind things up. After that, he could go back to Charleston and tell PawPaw the deed was done. Any debt his family owed one Eliza Chandler Edwards, direct descendant of old Elias Matthew Chandler of Crow Fly, in what had then been Oklahoma Territory, was finally settled.

The genealogist had done a great job in record time, running into a snag only at the point where Miss Chandler had married one James G. Edwards, born July 1, 1962, died September 7, 2001. It had been police research—in particular, the Financial Crimes Unit—that had dug up the fact that the lady and her husband had been involved a couple of years ago in a high-stakes investment scam. Edwards had gone down alone for that one—literally. Shot by one of his victims while out jogging, but before he died he had cleared his wife of any involvement. She'd never been linked directly to any illegal activities. Once cleared, she had hung around Dallas only long enough to liquidate her assets before dropping out of sight.

Beckett didn't know if she was guilty as sin or totally innocent. Didn't much care. He was doing this for PawPaw's sake, not hers.

In the end, it had been pure luck. Luck in the form of a reporter with an excellent visual memory who spent summer vacations on North Carolina's Outer Banks and who had happened to stop at a certain roadside stand on his drive south.

He'd called Carson from Nags Head. "Hey, man, weren't you checking out this Edwards woman a few weeks ago? The one that was mixed up in that scam out in Texas where all these old geezers got ripped off?"

And just like that, they'd had her. She'd holed up in the middle of nowhere with a gentleman named Frederick Grant, a great-uncle on her mother's side. Check and double-check. If it hadn't been for that one lucky break, it might've taken months. Beckett would've been tempted to pass the buck to the next generation, the way the men in his family had evidently been doing ever since the great-grandfather for whom he'd been named had cheated a business partner named Chandler out of his rightful share of Beckett money. Or so the story went.

At this point there was no next generation. Carson wasn't currently involved with anyone, and Beckett had taken one shot at it, missed by a mile, and been too gun-shy to try again.

Although he preferred to think of it as too busy.

"Money, the root of all evils," Beckett had mused when he'd checked in with his cousin Carson just before leaving Charleston that morning.

"Ain't that the truth? Wonder which side of the law old Lance would've been on if he'd lived in today's society."

"Hard to say. Mom dug up some old records, but they got soaked, pretty much ruined, during Hurricane Hugo." He'd politely suggested to his mother that a bank deposit box might be a better place to store valuable papers than a hot, leaky attic.

She'd responded, "It's not like they were family photographs. Besides, how was I to know they'd get wet and clump together? Now stop whining and taste this soup. I know butter's not supposed to be good for you, but I can hardly make Mama's crab bisque with margarine."

"Mom, I'm nearly forty years old, for cripes' sake. While I might occasionally comment on certain difficulties, I never whine. Hmm, a little more salt—maybe a tad more sherry?"

"That's what I thought, too. I know you don't, darling. Just look at you, you're turning grayer every time I see you."

According to his father, Beckett's mother's hair had turned white before she was even out of her teens.

All the girls in her high-school class had wanted gray hair. "It's one thing to turn gray when you're young enough to pass it off as a fashion statement. It's another thing when you're so old nobody gives it a second thought," she'd said more than once.

For the past fifteen or so years, her hair had been every shade of blond and red imaginable. At nearly sixty, she scarcely looked more than forty—forty-five, at the most.

"Honey, it's up to you how to handle it," she said as he helped himself to another spoonful of her famous soup, which contained shrimp as well as crab, plus enough cream and butter to clog every artery between Moncks Corner and Edisto Island. "PawPaw tried his best to find these people, but then he got sick."

Right. Beckett's grandfather, called PawPaw by family and friends alike, was as charming an old rascal as ever lived, but at the age of one hundred plus, he was still putting things off. Cheating the devil, he called it. When it came to buck passing, the Beckett men took a back seat to none.

Which is why some four generations after the "crime" had been committed, Beckett was trying to get the job done once and for all.

"What's the latest on the new tropical depression? You heard anything this morning?" Carson had asked.

"Pretty much stalled, last I heard. I hope to God it doesn't strengthen—I've got half a dozen ships in the North Atlantic using the new tracking device. They all start dodging hurricanes, I'm going to be pretty busy trying to find out if any of them are being hijacked.''

"Yeah, well…take a break. Go play fairy godfather for a change."

"Easy for you to say."

When his mother had called to say that PawPaw had had another stroke, Beckett had been in the middle of negotiations with an Irish chemical tanker company that had been hijacked often enough for the owners to feel compelled to contact his firm, Beckett Marine Risk Management, Inc. "Just a teeny-weeny stroke this time, but he really would like to see you and Carson." She'd gone on to say she didn't know how long he could hang on, but seeing his two grandsons would mean the world to him.

Beckett came home. And, as Carson was still out of commission, it was Beckett who'd gotten stuck with the assignment.

So now here he was, chasing an elusive lady who had recently been spotted selling produce and God knows what else at a roadside stand in the northeast corner of North Carolina.

"PawPaw, you owe me big-time for this." Beckett loved his grandfather. Hadn't seen much of him recently, but he intended to rectify that if the old guy would just pull through this latest setback. Family, he was belatedly coming to realize, was one part anchor, one part compass. In rough weather, he'd hate to be caught at sea without either one.

So, maybe in a year or so, he thought as he crossed

the state line between North Carolina and Virginia, he might consider relocating. He'd incorporated in Delaware because of its favorable laws, but that didn't mean he had to stay there. After a while, a man got tired of zigzagging across too many time zones.

Pulling up at a stoplight, he yawned, rubbed his bristly jaw and wished he had a street address. He'd called ahead to rent a four-wheel-drive vehicle in case the chase involved more than the five-lane highway that ran from Virginia to North Carolina's Outer Banks. Having experienced back roads of all descriptions from Zaire to Kuala Lumpur, he knew better than to take anything for granted. So far it looked like a pretty straight shot, but he'd learned to be prepared for almost anything.

"We're out of prunes," came a wavering lament from the back of the house.

"Look in the pantry," Liza called. "They've changed the name—they're called dried plums now, but they're still the same thing." She smiled as she snapped her cash box shut and tied a calico apron over her T-shirt and tan linen pants. Uncle Fred—her great-uncle, really—was still sharp as a tack at the age of eighty-six, but he didn't like it when things changed.

And things inevitably changed. In her case it had been a change for the better, she thought, looking around at the shabby-comfortable old room with its mail-order furniture and hand-crocheted antimacassars. A wobbly smoking stand, complete with humidor and pipe rack—although her uncle no longer smoked on orders from his physician—was now weighted down with all the farming and sports magazines he'd collected and never discarded. There was an air-conditioning unit in one of the windows, an ugly thing that blocked the view of the vacant lot on the other side, where someone evidently planned to build something. But until they could afford central air—which would be after the kitchen floor was replaced and the house reroofed—it served well enough. Both bedrooms had electric fans on the dressers, which made the humid August heat almost bearable.

Liza hadn't changed a thing when she'd moved in, other than to scrub the walls, floors and windows, wash all the linens and replace a few dry-rotted curtains when they'd fallen apart in her hands. Discount stores were marvelous places, she'd quickly discovered.

Shortly after she'd arrived, Liza had broken down and cried for the first time in months. She'd been cleaning the dead bugs from a closet shelf and had found a shoe box full of old letters and Christmas cards, including those she'd sent to Uncle Fred. Liza and her mother had always done the cards together, with Liza choosing them and her mother addressing the envelopes. Liza had continued to send Uncle Fred a card each year after her mother had died, never knowing whether or not they'd been received.

Dear, lonely Uncle Fred. She had taken a monumental chance, not even calling ahead to ask if she could come for a visit. She hadn't know anything about him, not really—just that he was her only living relative except for a cousin she hadn't seen in several years. She'd driven all the way across the country for a few days' visit, hoping—praying—she could stay until she could get her feet on the ground and plan her next step.

What was that old song about people who needed people?

They'd both been needy, not that either of them had ever expressed it in words. *We're out of prunes.* That was one of Uncle Fred's ways of letting her know he needed her. *Danged eyeglasses keep moving from where I put 'em.* That was another.

Life in this particular slow lane might lack a few of the amenities she'd once taken for granted, but she would willingly trade all the hot tubs and country clubs in the world for the quiet predictability she'd found here.

Not to mention the ability to see where every penny came from and where and how it was spent. She might once have been negligent—criminally negligent, some would say—but after the lessons she'd been forced to learn, she'd become a fanatic about documenting every cent they took in. Her books, such as they were, balanced to the penny.

When she'd arrived in May of last year, Uncle Fred had been barely hanging on, relying on friends and neighbors to supply him with surplus produce. People would stop by occasionally to buy a few vegetables, leaving the money in a bowl on the counter. They made their own change, and she seriously doubted if it ever occurred to him to count and see if he was being cheated. What would he have done about it? Threaten them with his cane?

Gradually, as her visit stretched out over weeks and then months, she had instigated small changes. By the end of the year, it was taken for granted that she would stay. No words were necessary. He'd needed her and she'd needed him—needed even more desperately to be needed, although her self-esteem had been so badly damaged she hadn't realized it at the time.

Uncle Fred still insisted on being present every day, even though he seldom got out of his rocking chair anymore. She encouraged his presence because she thought it was good for him. The socializing. He'd said once that all his friends had moved to a nursing home or gone to live with relatives.

She'd said something to the effect that in his case, the relative had come to live with him. He'd chuckled. He had a nice laugh, his face going all crinkly, his eyes hidden behind layers of wrinkles under his bushy white brows.

For the most part, the people who stopped for the free ice water and lingered to buy produce were pleasant. Maybe it was the fact that they were on vacation, or maybe it was simply because when Uncle Fred was holding court, he managed to strike up a conversation with almost everyone who stopped by. Seated in his ancient green porch rocker, in bib overalls, his Romeo slippers and Braves baseball cap, with his cane hidden behind the cooler, he greeted them all with a big smile and a drawled, "How-de-do, where y'all from?"

Now and then, after the stand closed down for the day, she would drive him to Bay View to visit his friends while she went on to do the grocery shopping. Usually he was waiting for her when she got back, grumbling about computers. "All they talk about— them computer things. Good baseball game right there on the TV set and all they want to talk about is going on some kind of a web. Second childhood, if you ask me."

So they hadn't visited as much lately. He seemed content at home, and that pleased her enormously. Granted, Liza thought as she broke open a roll of pennies, they would never get rich. But then, getting rich had been the last thing on her mind when she'd fled across country from the chaos her life had become. All she asked was that they sell enough to stay in business, more for Uncle Fred's sake than her own. She could always get a job; the classified ads were full of help-wanted ads in the summertime. But Fred Grant was another matter. She would never forget how he'd welcomed her that day last May when she'd turned up on his doorstep.

"Salina's daughter, you say? All the way from Texas? Lord bless ye, young'un, you've got the family look, all right. Set your suitcase in the front room, it's got a brand-new mattress."

The mattress might have been brand-new at one time, but that didn't mean it was comfortable. Still, beggars couldn't be choosers, and at that point in her life, she'd been a beggar. Now, she was proud to say, she earned her own way. Slowly, one step at a time, but every step was straightforward, documented and scrupulously honest.

"I'll be outside if you need me," she called now as she headed out the front door. Fred Grant had his pride. It would take him at least five minutes to negotiate the uneven flagstone path between the house and the tin-roofed stand he'd established nearly forty years ago when he'd hurt his back and was no longer able to farm.

Gradually he and his wife had sold off all the land, hanging on to the house and the half acre it sat on. Fred ruefully admitted they had wasted the money on a trip to the Grand Ole Opry in Nashville and a fur coat for his wife. He had buried her in it a few years later.

Now he and Liza had each other. Gradually she had settled into this quiet place, far from the ruins of the glamorous, fast-paced life that had suited James far more than it had ever suited her.

By liquidating practically everything she possessed before she'd headed here—the art, her jewelry and the outrageously expensive clothes she would never again wear—she had managed to pay off a few of James's victims and their lawyers. She'd given her maid, Patty Ann Garrett, a Waterford potpourri jar she'd always admired. She would have given her more, for she genuinely liked the girl, but she'd felt honor bound to pay back as much of what James had stolen as she could.

Besides, her clothes would never fit Patty Ann, who was five foot four, with a truly amazing bust size. In contrast, Liza was tall, skinny and practically flat. James had called her figure classy, which she'd found wildly amusing at the time.

For a woman with a perfectly good college degree, never mind that it wasn't particularly marketable, she'd been incredibly ignorant. She was learning, though. Slowly, steadily, she was learning how to take care of herself and someone who was even needier than she was.

"Good morning…yes, those are grown right here in Currituck County." She would probably say the same words at least a hundred times on a good day. Someone—the Tourist Bureau, probably—had estimated that traffic passing through on summer Saturdays alone would be roughly 45,000 people. People on their way to and from the beach usually stopped at the larger markets, but Uncle Fred had his share of regulars, some of whom said they'd first stopped by as children with their parents.

After Labor Day, the people who stopped seemed to take more time to look around. A few even offered suggestions on how to improve her business. It was partly those suggestions and partly Liza's own creativity she credited for helping revitalize her uncle's small roadside stand, which had been all but defunct when she'd shown up. First she'd bought the second-hand cooler and put up a sign advertising free ice water, counting on the word *free* to bring in a few customers. Then she'd found a source of rag dolls, hand-woven scatter rugs and appliquéd canvas tote bags. She'd labeled them shell bags, and they sold as fast as she could get in a new supply. Last fall she'd added a few locally grown cured hams. By the time they'd closed for the winter, business had more than doubled.

Now, catching a whiff of Old Spice mingled with the earthy smell of freshly dug potatoes and sweet onions, she glanced up as Uncle Fred settled into his rocker. "You should have worn your straw hat today—that cap won't protect your ears or the back of your neck."

The morning sun still slanted under the big water oaks. "Put on your own bonnet, woman. I'm tougher'n stroppin' leather, but skin like yours weren't meant to fry."

"Bonnets. Hmm. I wonder if we could get one of the women to make us a few old-fashioned sunbonnets. What do you bet they'd catch on?" Mark of a good businesswoman, she thought proudly. Always thinking ahead.

She sold three cabbages, half a dozen cantaloupes and a hand-loomed scatter rug the first hour, then perched on her stool and watched the traffic flow past. When a dark green SUV pulled onto the graveled parking area, she stood, saying quietly to her uncle, "What do you think, country ham?" When business was slow they sometimes played the game of trying to guess in advance who would buy what.

Together they watched the tall, tanned man approach. His easy way of moving belied the silver-gray of his thick hair. He couldn't be much past forty, she decided. Dye his hair and he could pass for thirty. "Maybe just a glass of ice water," she murmured. He didn't strike her as a typical vacationer, much less one who was interested in produce.

"That 'un's selling, not buying. Got that look in his eye."

Beckett took his time approaching the tall, thin woman with the wraparound calico apron, the sunstruck auburn hair and the fashion model's face. If this was the same woman who'd been involved in a high-stakes con game that covered three states and involved a few offshore banking institutions, what the hell was she doing in a place like this?

And if this wasn't Eliza Chandler Edwards, then what the devil was a woman with her looks doing sitting behind a bin of onions, with Grandpaw Cranket or Crocket or whatever the guy's name was, rocking and grinning behind her.

"How-de-do? Where ye from, son?"

"Beg pardon?" He paused between a display of green stuff and potatoes.

"We get a lot of reg'lars stopping by, but I don't believe I've seen you before. You from up in Virginia?"

"It's a rental car, Uncle Fred," the woman said quietly.

Beckett tried to place her accent and found he couldn't quite pin it down. Cultured Southern was about as close as he could come. She was tall, at least five-nine or -ten. Her bone structure alone would have made her a world-class model if she could manage to walk without tripping over her feet. He was something of a connoisseur when it came to women; he'd admired any number of them from a safe distance. If this was the woman he'd worked so damned hard to track down, the question still applied—what the devil was she doing here selling produce?

He nodded to the old man and concentrated on the woman. ''Ms. Edwards?''

Liza felt a gaping hole open up in her chest. Did she know him? She managed to catch her breath, but she couldn't stop staring. There was something about him that riveted her attention. His eyes, his hands— even his voice. If she'd ever met him before, she would have remembered. ''I'm afraid you've made a mistake.''

''You're not Eliza Chandler Edwards?''

Uncle Fred was frowning now, fumbling behind the cooler for his cane. Oh, Lord, Liza thought, if he tried to come to her rescue, they'd both end up in trouble. She had told him a little about her past when she'd first arrived, but nothing about the recent hang-up calls, much less the letter that had come last month.

''I believe you have the advantage,'' she murmured, stalling for time. How could he possibly know who she was? She was legally Eliza Jackson Chandler again, wiping out the last traces of her disastrous marriage.

''Could I have a glass of that free ice water you're advertising?''

On a morning when both the temperature and the humidity hovered in the low nineties, this man looked cool as the proverbial cucumber. Not a drop of sweat dampened that high, tanned brow. "Of course. Right over there." Indicating the container of plastic cups, Liza fought to maintain her composure.

When he tipped back his head to swallow, her gaze followed the movement of his throat. His brand of fitness hadn't come from any gym, she'd be willing to bet on it. Nor had that tan been acquired over a single weekend at the beach. The contrast of bronzed skin with pewter hair, ice-gray eyes and winged black eyebrows was startling, not to mention strikingly attractive.

The word *sexy* came to mind, and she immediately pushed it away. Sex was the very last thing that concerned her now. Getting rid of this man overshadowed everything.

But first she needed to know if he was the one who'd been stalking her—if not literally, then figuratively, by calling her in the middle of the night and hanging up. Just last month she'd received a letter addressed to her by name at Uncle Fred's rural route box number. The return address was a post office box in South Dallas. Inside the plain white envelope had been a blank sheet of paper.

"I don't believe you answered my question," he said, his voice deep, slightly rough edged, but not actually threatening. At least, not yet.

"First, I'd like to know who's asking." She would see his demand and raise him one.

"Beckett. L. Jones Beckett."

"That still doesn't explain why you're here asking questions, Mr. Beckett." If that really is your name.

"The name doesn't ring any bells?"

Liza turned away to stare down at a display of summer squash. Had any of James's victims been named Beckett? She honestly couldn't recall, there had been so many. With the help of her lawyer, she'd done the best she could to make amends, but even after liquidating everything there still hadn't been enough to go around. Of course the lawyers, including her divorce lawyer, whom she'd no longer needed at that point, had taken a large cut of all she'd been able to raise.

He was still waiting for an answer. "No, I'm sorry. Should it?"

"My grandfather was Lancelot Elias Beckett."

"He has my sympathy." Her arms were crossed over her breasts, but they failed to warm her inside, where it counted. Uncle Fred, bless his valorous heart, had stopped rocking and stopped smiling. His cane was at the ready, across his bony knees.

Two

This was the one. Beckett was certain of it. Otherwise, why was she so skittish? A simple farmer's daughter selling her wares on a country road, no matter how stunning she might be, would hardly slam the door shut on a potential customer.

And she'd slammed it shut, all right. Battened down the hatches and all but thrown open the gun ports. *Guarded* didn't begin to describe the look in those whiskey-brown eyes. *Frightened* came closer.

But frightened of what? Being brought in for questioning again?

So far as he knew, that particular case had been closed when her husband had taken the fall. She'd been a material witness, but they'd never been able to tie anything directly to her—even though she'd still been legally married to Edwards when he'd been shot in the throat by a man who'd been bled dry by one of his shell games. The victim, poor devil, had returned the favor.

"Not from Virginia, are ye?" the old man asked, causing them both to turn and stare. His smile was as bland as the summer sky. The brass-headed cane was nowhere in sight.

"Uh...South Carolina. Mostly," Beckett admitted. He'd lived in the state of his birth for exactly eighteen years. He still kept his school yearbooks, his athletic trophies and fishing gear at his parents' home, for lack of space in his own apartment.

The old man nodded. "I figgered South C'lina or Georgia. Got a good ear for placing where folks is from."

"What do you want?" It was the woman this time. Her eyes couldn't have looked more wary if he'd been a snake she'd found in one of her fancy canvas bags.

Under other circumstances, he might have been interested in following up on her question. Her looks were an intriguing blend of Come Hither and Back Off. "Nothing," he told her. "I have something for you, though." What he had was a worthless, mostly illegible bundle of paper. He'd left the money in his briefcase in the truck. If she wasn't the right one, the papers wouldn't mean anything to her, and if she was...

She was. He'd lay odds on it.

But she wasn't ready to drop her guard. "Something you want me to sell for you? Sorry, we deal only with locals.''

Irritated, he snapped back, "Just some papers for now. Look, if you'll give me a minute to explain—''

She jammed her fists in her apron pockets and stepped back against the counter. "No. You can keep your papers. I refuse to accept them. You're a…a process server, aren't you?'' She had a face that could be described as beautiful, elegant—even patrician. That didn't keep her from squaring up that delicate jaw of hers like an amateur boxer bracing for a round-house punch.

For some reason it got to him. "I am not a process server. I am not a deputy, nor am I a bounty hunter. I'm not a reporter, either, in case you were worried.'' In his line of work, patience was a requisite. Occasionally his ran short. "I was asked to locate you in order to give you something that's rightfully yours. At least, it belonged to a relative of yours.'' Might as well set her curiosity to working for him. "I might add that I've had one devil of a time tracking you down.''

If anything, she looked even more suspicious. Considering what her husband had been involved in, maybe she had just cause. But dammit, if he was willing to fork over ten grand from his own personal bank account, the least she could do was accept it. A gracious thank-you wouldn't be too far out of line, either.

"Why don't I just leave this packet with you and you can glance through it at your leisure.'' He held out an oversize manila envelope.

Liza jammed her fists deeper into the pockets of her apron. At her *leisure?* No way. He might not be a process server—she'd never heard of one of those who suggested anyone examine their papers at her leisure—but that didn't make him any less of a threat. Lawsuits were a dime a dozen these days, and there were plenty of aggrieved parties who might think they had a case against her, just because she'd been married to James and had benefited from the money he'd swindled.

Benefited in the short run, at least.

Before she could get rid of him—politely or otherwise—a car pulled up and two couples and three kids piled out.

"Mama, can I have—"

"I've got to go to the bathroom, Aunt Ruth."

"My, would you look at them onions. Are they as sweet as Videlias, Miss?"

Forcing a smile, Liza stepped behind the homemade counter, with its ancient manual cash register surrounded by the carefully arranged displays of whatever needed moving before it passed its prime.

"Those are from the Lake Mattamuskeet area." She gestured in the general direction of neighboring Hyde County. "They're so sweet and mild you could almost eat them like apples."

She explained to the round-faced woman wearing blue jeans, faux diamond earrings and rubber flipflops that there were no bathroom facilities, but there were rest rooms at the service station less than a mile down the road. Uncle Fred still referred to the five-lane highway as "the road."

While she was adding up purchases, two more customers stopped by. Uncle Fred engaged one of the men in a conversation about his favorite baseball team. Finding a fellow baseball fan always made his day.

"Does that thing really work?" One of the women nodded to her cash register.

"Works just fine, plus it helps keep my utility bills down." It was her stock answer whenever anyone commented on her low-tech equipment. Although what they expected of a roadside stand, she couldn't imagine. She weighed a sack of shelled butter beans on the hanging scales.

"I saw something like that once on the *Antiques Roadshow*," the woman marveled.

From the corner of her eye, Liza watched the stranger leave. Actually caught herself admiring his lean backside as he sauntered toward his SUV. Curiosity nudged her, but only momentarily. Attractive men—even unattractive men—who knew her name or anything at all about her, she could well do without.

He started the engine, but didn't drive off. Through the tinted windshield, he appeared to be talking on a cell phone.

Who was he? What did he want from her? *Just leave me alone, damn you! I don't have anything more to give!*

After James had been indicted, one distraught woman had actually tracked her down to show her a picture of the home she had lost when her husband had invested every cent they had saved in one of James's real-estate scams. She'd been crying. Liza had ended up crying, too. She'd given the woman a diamond-and-sapphire bracelet, which certainly wouldn't buy her a new home, but it was all she could do at the time.

To her heartfelt relief, the dark green SUV pulled out and drove off. For a few blessed moments she and Uncle Fred were alone. The midday heat brought a bloom of moisture to her face despite the fact that she still felt cold and shaky inside. She opened two diet colas and handed one to her uncle. She was wondering idly if she should bring one of the electric fans from the house when she spotted the manila envelope.

Well, shoot. She was tempted to leave it where it was, on the far corner of the counter, weighted down with a rutabaga.

Uncle Fred hitched his chair deeper into the shade and resumed rocking. "Funny, that fellow wanting to give you something. What you reckon it was?"

"Some kind of papers, he said." She nodded to the envelope that was easily visible from where she sat, but not from the other side of the counter.

"Maybe we won the lottery." It was a standing joke. Every now and then her uncle would mention driving up into Virginia and buying lottery tickets. They never had. Uncle Fred had surrendered his driver's license a decade ago after his pickup had died, and Liza didn't want anything she hadn't earned. If someone told her where a pot of gold was buried, she'd hand over a shovel and wish them luck.

"I guess I'd better start stringing beans while things are quiet. I'll freeze another batch tonight." She froze whatever didn't sell before it passed its prime. Her uncle called it laying by for the winter. It had a solid, comfortable sound.

"Aren't you going to see what's in the envelope?"

"Ta-dah! The envelope, please." She tried to turn it into a joke, but she had that sick feeling again— the same feeling that had started the day James's so-called investment business had begun to unravel. At first she'd thought—actually hoped—that the feeling of nausea meant she was pregnant.

Thank God it hadn't.

"Here comes another car." She handed her uncle the envelope and moved behind the counter. "Help yourself if you're curious."

There wasn't much choice when it came to a place to stay. He could've driven on to the beach, but common sense told Beckett that on a Saturday in late August, his chances of finding a vacancy weren't great. Besides, he wasn't finished with Queen Eliza. By now she would have looked over the papers and realized he was on the level, even if she didn't yet understand what it was all about. The name Chandler was easy enough to read, even in century-old faded ink. Add to that the letter from his grandfather, Elias Beckett—funny, the coincidence of the names. Elias Chandler and Elias Beckett. Two different generations, though, if the genealogist had the straight goods.

At any rate, he would go back after she'd closed up shop for the day to answer any questions she might have and hand over the money. Meanwhile, he could arrange to see a couple of potential clients at Newport News Shipyard. Things had clamped down so tight after September 11 that it practically took an act of Congress to get through security.

Fortunately, he had clearance there. He'd make a few calls and, with any luck, be on his way back to Charleston by tomorrow afternoon. He would spend a few days with his parents before heading back to Dublin to wind up negotiations with the tanker firm.

The important thing was to set PawPaw's mind at ease. If, as he'd been given to understand, the Becketts owed the Chandlers money, he would willingly pay it back. In exchange, however, he wanted a signed receipt and the understanding that any future heirs would be notified that the debt had been settled. A gentleman's agreement might have served in PawPaw's day—not that it had served the original Chandler very well. But in today's litigious society, he preferred something more tangible.

After that, he didn't care what she did with the money. She could buy herself a decent cooler and a cash register that didn't date back to the thirties or get herself a grind organ and a monkey for all he cared. He'd been given a mission, and he'd come too far not to carry it out. But he could hardly ask for a signed receipt for ten thousand dollars while she was busy weighing out sixty-nine cents' worth of butter beans.

"Over to you, lady," he said softly, setting up his laptop on the fake mahogany table in his motel room. He placed his cell phone beside it, tossed his briefcase on the bed, set the air-conditioning for Arctic blast and peeled off his sweat-damp shirt. He'd stayed in far better places; he'd stayed in far worse. At least the room was clean and there was a decent-size shower and reasonably comfortable bed. Slipping off his shoes, he waited for the phone call to go through.

"Car? Beckett. Yeah, I found her right where your friend said she'd be. Tell him I owe him a steak dinner, will you?" He went on to describe the place, including the old man she was apparently living with. "Great-uncle on her mother's side, according to the genealogist's chart. Looks like he could use a few bucks. The house is listing about five degrees to the northeast."

Carson congratulated him. "When you headed back this way?"

"Tomorrow, probably. I'd like to handle some business in the Norfolk area as long as I'm this close. Maybe stop off in Morehead City on the way and be back in Charleston by tomorrow night."

"Want me to call Aunt Becky and let her know?"

"Wait until I know for sure when I'll be heading back again. I ran into a small snag."

"Don't tell me she's the wrong Chandler."

"She's the right Chandler, I'm pretty sure of that. Trouble is, she doesn't want to accept the papers."

"Doesn't want to accept *ten grand?*"

"We never got that far. I gave her the papers, but she needs to look 'em over before I hand over the money. Or at least as much as she can decipher."

"Didn't you explain what it was about?"

"I was going to, but she got tied up with customers before I had a chance to do any explaining. I didn't feel like hanging around all day. I'll go back later on, after the place closes down and explain what it's all about. Listen, did it ever occur to you that if she starts figuring out the rate of inflation over the past hundred or so years, we might have a problem on our hands?"

"Nope, never occurred to me. Sorry you mentioned it, but look—we don't really know how much money was involved originally, do we?"

Beckett idly scratched a mosquito bite. "Good point. I'm going to ask for a receipt, though. You think that's going too far?"

"Hey, you're the guy who deals with government regulations and red tape. Me, I'm just a lowly cop."

He was a bit more than that, but Beckett knew what he meant. He didn't want the next generation of Becketts to trip on any legal loopholes. Before he handed over the money, he would definitely get her signature on a release.

"You know, Bucket," Carson mused, "it occurs to me that the way we're doing this, we could end up in trouble if old man Chandler scattered too many seeds. Just because we were only able to locate two heirs, that doesn't necessarily mean there aren't any more."

"Don't remind me. That's one of the reasons I want things sewed up with lawyer-proof thread. You can handle the next contender however you want to. If any more turn up after that, we'll flash our receipt and send them to Ms. Edwards and what's-her-name—the other one. They can share the spoils…or not."

After answering a few questions about various family members, Beckett stripped down and headed for the shower. He started out with a hot deluge and let it run cold. The hot water eased the ache caused by too many hours strapped into a bucket seat, while the cool water helped clear his mind. As he slathered soap from the postage-stamp-size bar onto his flat midriff and let the suds trickle down his torso, the image of Eliza Chandler Edwards arose in his mind.

Lancelot Beckett had known his share of beautiful women—maybe more than his share; although, ever since he'd been left at the altar at the impressionable age of twenty-two, he'd made it a policy never to invite a repetition. At this point in his life he figured it was too late, anyhow. Any man who wasn't married by his midthirties probably wasn't a viable candidate.

All the same, it had been a long time since he'd met a more intriguing woman than Ms. Edwards. Skilled at reading people, he hadn't missed the flash of interest that had flickered in those golden-brown eyes just before wariness had shut it off. Pit that against the physical barriers she'd erected and, yeah…*intriguing* wasn't too strong a word. Her hair was not quite brown, not quite red. Thick and wavy, with a scattering of golden strands that had a tendency to curl, she wore it twisted up on her head and anchored down with some kind of a tortoiseshell gadget. Her clothes were the kind deliberately designed to conceal rather than reveal. He wondered if she realized that on the right woman, concealment was a hell of a lot more exciting than full exposure.

Oh, yeah, she was something all right. Everything about her shouted, "Look but don't touch."

In fact, don't even bother to look. Which had the reverse effect. Did she know that? Was it deliberate?

Somehow he didn't think so.

He adjusted the water temperature again, trying for ice-cold, but only getting tepid. Not for the first time he told himself he should have waited and let Carson do the honors. Car was two years younger and didn't have quite as much rough mileage on him as Beckett did.

But he'd promised. As his mother had stated flatly, time was running out, and it was time to lay this business to rest once and for all. "PawPaw's worried sick, and Coley doesn't need that kind of aggravation."

Ever since Beckett's father had been diagnosed with emphysema, his mother's main purpose in life had been to spare him anything more stressful than choosing which pair of socks to wear with his madras Bermudas when he got up in the morning.

She'd been waiting at the airport when Beckett had flown in more than a week ago. She'd hugged him fiercely, then stepped back to give him her patented Inspector Mother's once-over. Nodding in approval, she said, "You do this one thing for me, honey, then you come back here and tell PawPaw it's finished. Just find somebody named Chandler and hand over that mess of old papers and whatever else you think the Becketts owe them, then you can go back to chasing your pirates. Honestly, of all things for a grown man to be doing." She'd tsk-tsked him and slid in under the wheel.

Beckett had tried several times to explain to his mother that piracy on the high seas was as prevalent now as it had been in the days when Blackbeard had plied his trade off the Carolina coast. No matter. To her, it was still a kid's game. She'd wanted him to go into politics like his state senator father, Coley Jefferson Beckett. Or into investment banking like his grandfather, Elias Lancelot Beckett, and his great-grandfather, L. Frederick Beckett—the man who had started this whole bloody mess.

A few years ago he had fallen hard for a sexy marine biologist named Carolyn. Fallen hard but, as usual, not quite hard enough. After about six months he'd been the one to call it quits. He'd done it as graciously as he knew how, but Carolyn had been hurt. Beckett had readily accepted his guilt. Fortunately—or perhaps not—his work made it easy to run from commitment.

The payback had come a year later when he'd run into a glowing and very pregnant Carolyn and her professor husband at a jazz festival. He'd had a few bad moments as a result, wondering if he might have made a mistake. Family had always been important to him. Even seeing that old man today, rocking away the last years of his life at a roadside produce stand, had reminded him a little too much of his own mortality.

True, the Beckett men were generally long-lived, but what would it be like to grow old completely alone, with no wife to warm his bed—no kids to drive him nuts? No grandkids to crawl up on his arthritic knees?

His only legacy was a healthy portfolio and a small, modestly successful firm he'd built from practically nothing—one that included a two-room office in Delaware, a partner and a part-time secretary. His will left whatever worldly goods he possessed at the time of his death to his parents. Who else was there? Carson? A few distant cousins he'd never even met?

Cripes, now he really was getting depressed. Maybe it was all this humidity—he was coming down with a bad case of mildew of the brain, he told himself, only half joking as he crossed the bedroom buck stark naked to dig out a change of clothes.

On the other hand, it could be due to the fact that he hadn't eaten anything since the lousy chili dog he'd bought at the airport. One cup of free ice water didn't do the job.

Liza washed her hair and towel dried it before fixing supper. Then she did something she hadn't done in a long, long time. She stood in front of the fogged and age-speckled mirror on her dresser and studied her naked body. James had called her classy. Any man in his right mind would call her clinically emaciated. Her hipbones poked out, her ribs were clearly visible, and as for her breasts...

Tentatively she covered the slight swells with her hands. Her nipples, still sensitive from the rough toweling, nudged her palms, and she cursed under her breath and turned away.

That part of her life was over. Fortunately, sex had never played that large a role. After the first year or so, she had done her wifely duty once a week, sometimes twice, and then even that had ended. They'd gone out almost every night, entertaining or being entertained, and by the time they got home, they'd both been ready to fall into bed. To sleep, not to play. After a few drinks James hadn't been up to it, and she'd felt more relief than anything else.

Dressing hastily, she hurried into the kitchen. There was a Braves game tonight; they were playing the Mets. Next to the Yankees, the Mets were her uncle's favorite team to hate. Once the dishes were washed she could retire to her room and look through those blasted papers. It wouldn't hurt. The envelope wasn't sealed, just fastened with a metal clasp. If it had anything to do with James, she would simply toss it, because that part of her life was over and done with. She had repaid as much as she was able, although she hadn't been obligated to do even that much. She'd been cleared of all responsibility after James had made it quite clear before he'd died that she'd never even known what was going on, much less been involved.

His last act had been one of surprising generosity, but that didn't mean she hadn't been brought in for questioning. Nor did the fact that she hadn't known what was going on mean she'd escaped feeling guilty once she'd found out. She'd lived high on the hog, as Uncle Fred would say, for almost eleven years on the proceeds of James's financial shell games. The beautiful house in North Dallas, the trips to all those island resorts that James always claimed were for networking. Like a blind fool, she'd gone along whenever he'd asked her to; although, for the most part, she hadn't particularly liked the people he'd met there.

When the dishes were done, she turned out the light. Uncle Fred called from the living room. "Game time. You want to bet on the spread?"

"A quarter says the Mets win by five points." She knew little about baseball and wasn't particularly interested, but he enjoyed the games so much that she tried to share his enthusiasm.

"You're on! I know you, gal—you like that Piazza feller that catches for 'em." His teasing was a part of the ritual.

Liza leaned against the door frame and watched him prepare for the night's entertainment: fruit bowl nearby, recliner in position and a bag of potato chips hidden under the smoking stand. She was turning to go to her room when headlights sprayed across the front window. Traffic out on the highway didn't do that, not unless a car turned in.

"Uncle Fred, did you invite anyone over to watch the game?"

But her uncle had turned up the volume. Either he didn't hear or was pretending not to, so it was left to Liza to see who'd come calling. Occasionally one of the women who supplied the soft goods would drop off work on the way to evening prayer meeting. But this was Saturday, not Wednesday.

She knew who it was, even before he climbed out of the SUV parked under one of the giant oaks. She checked to be sure the screen was hooked, then waited for him to reach the front porch. He'd instructed her to look over the papers and said he'd see her later. She'd thought later meant tomorrow—or, better yet, never.

Doing nothing more threatening than sauntering up the buckled flagstone walk, the man looked dangerous. Something about the way he moved. Not like an athlete, exactly—more like a predator. Dark, deceptively attractive, moving silently through the deepening shadows.

Get a grip, woman.

"Let me guess," she said when he came up onto the porch. She made no move to unhook the screen door. "You came to tell me I won the Publisher's Sweepstakes."

"Have you had chance to look over what I left you?"

"Not yet." She refused to turn on the porch light because it attracted moths and mosquitoes. Besides, it wasn't quite dark yet. But it didn't take much light to delineate those angular cheekbones, that arrogant blade of a nose and the mouth that managed to be firm and sexy at the same time.

Listen to you, Eliza, would you just stop it?

"Then how about reading them now? It shouldn't take long. Unfortunately, most of the pages have stuck together, but once you've skimmed the top layer or so, I'll explain anything you don't understand and hand over the money. Then you can sign a release and I'll leave."

"I'm not signing anything, I'm not buying anything, I'm not—" She frowned. "What money?"

"Give me three minutes, I'll try to talk fast. Are you or are you not the great-granddaughter of Elias Matthew Chandler, of...uh, Crow Fly, in Oklahoma Territory?"

Her jaw fell. Her eyes narrowed. "Are you crazy?"

Beckett slapped a mosquito on his neck. "Man, they're bloodthirsty little devils, aren't they? Any reports of West Nile virus around these parts?"

She shoved the screen door open, deliberately bumping it against his foot. "Oh, for goodness' sake, come inside. You've got two minutes left to tell me why you're harassing me."

He took a deep breath. Liza couldn't help noticing the size and breadth of his chest under shoulders that were equally impressive. Not that she was impressed. Still, a woman couldn't help but notice any man who looked as good and smelled as good and—

Well, shoot! "One minute and thirty seconds," she warned.

"Time out. You still haven't answered my question."

"You haven't answered mine, either. All right then, yes, I might be related to someone who might originally have been from Oklahoma. However, I don't happen to have a copy of my pedigree, so if whatever you're trying to prove involves my lineage, you'd better peddle your papers somewhere else. One minute and counting."

"I have." His smile packed a wallop, even if she didn't trust him.

"You have what? Tried peddling your papers somewhere else?" And then, unable to slam the door on her curiosity, she said, "What money? Is this a sweepstakes thing?"

"You might say that." The smile was gone, but the effect of those cool gray eyes was undiminished. "Would you by any chance have a cousin named Kathryn, uh—Dixon?"

Some of the wind went out of her sails. From the living room, her uncle cackled and called out, "Better get in here, missy—your team just struck out again."

"Look, would you please just say whatever you have to say and leave? I don't know much about my family history, so if you're trying to prove we're related, you'd do better to check with someone else who knows more about it than I do. And if you're after anything else, I'm not interested." Never mind the money. She knew better than anyone not to fall for the old "something for nothing" dodge.

The man who called himself L. Jones Beckett

edged past her until he could look into the living room. "Is that the Braves-Mets game? What's the score?"

"So you're back, are ye? Thought ye might be. General Sherman's not going to be taking Atlanta tonight, no siree. Score's one to one, the South's winning."

Liza closed her eyes and groaned. If he could talk baseball, she would never get rid of him. Uncle Fred would see to that. She might as well read his damned papers and be done with it.

Three

"**B**ring Mr. Beckett a glass of iced tea, Liza-girl. Have some potato chips, son." Suddenly Uncle Fred leaned forward, glaring at the screen. "What do you mean, strike? That pitch was outside by a gol-darn mile!"

Liza left them to their game and headed down the hall to her bedroom. She would skim whatever it was he insisted she read, hand it back to him and show him the door, and that would be the end of that. If he did happen to be peddling some kind of get-rich-quick scheme, he'd come knocking on the wrong door this time. Any junk mail that even hinted that she was a big winner got tossed without ever getting opened. She didn't want one red cent unless she knew exactly where it had come from.

The papers slid out in a clump. For a moment she only stared at them lying there on her white cotton bedspread. They looked as if they'd been soaked in tea. The top sheet appeared to be a letter, so she started with that.

"My Dear Eli..."

Liza made out that much before the ink faded. The ornate script was difficult to read, even without the faded ink and the work of generations of silverfish. She squinted at the date on the barely legible heading. September...was that *1900?* Mercy! Someone should have taken better care of it, whether or not it was valuable. Maybe the writer was someone important. If it had been a baseball card from that era—if they'd even had baseball cards back then—her uncle would have done backflips, arthritis or not.

She gave up halfway down the page after making out a word here, a few words there. Whoever had written the letter more than a hundred years ago appeared to be bragging about making loads of money on something or other, but the script was too ornate, the ink too faded, the insect damage too great, to make out more than a few random lines.

Judging by the fancy borders, the rest of the papers appeared to be certificates of some sort. They were so fragile she didn't dare risk prying them apart. In a separate clump were a few sheets that looked as if they might have been torn from a ledger. The only words she could make out were "Merchants Bank" and "deposit to the..." Amount of? Account of? Something that looked like shorehavers.

Shorehavers? Shaveholders?

"Shareholders," she murmured aloud, "500 shares of..."

Whatever the name of the company, whatever the value of the stock, an army of silverfish had successfully obliterated the record.

And then she caught her breath. That creep! That slow-talking, smooth-walking creep!

Oh, sure. He'd found these valuable-looking certificates, but before they could go up for sale they needed to be authenticated by an expert. Wasn't that the way it was supposed to go? Only poor Mr. Beckett, if that really was his name, couldn't quite swing it alone. He was willing to cut her in, however, for the small sum of, say five hundred dollars—a thousand would be even better if she could scrape it up—to have the certificates authenticated. As earnest money, he would toss in an equal amount.

How many suckers had he talked into investing in his scheme? It was a classic street con. The found wallet. The pocketbook left in a phone booth.

What she ought to do was turn this jerk over to the sheriff.

From the front of the house she heard a roar. Baseball fans were an excitable lot. Her uncle shouted, "Go it, son! Show them fellers how it's done!"

Evidently one of the Braves had hit a home run. She only hoped L. J. Beckett enjoyed the baseball game, because his other game wasn't going to play. Not tonight. Not with her.

Before leaving her room, she shook down her hair,

gave it a few swipes with the hairbrush and then fastened it back up again, tighter than ever. It was more a security thing than a matter of style or even comfort. James used to call her a throwback to a time when women over a certain age wore their hair pinned up. Only their husbands had the privilege of seeing them with their hair hanging down their backs. Now, every Tom, Dick and Harry had the privilege of seeing any woman of any age with her hair down.

Okay, so maybe she was a throwback. Or maybe she was instinctively searching for a safer time.

Fat chance.

She'd put on a clean pair of jeans after her bath, along with a T-shirt that was now damp where she'd splashed it washing dishes. Hardly her most flattering outfit, but then, she wasn't out to impress anyone. Especially not some silver-haired devil who thought he had her number.

"Are we still winning?" She addressed her uncle, but handed the envelope back to the visitor.

He ignored her outstretched hand. He'd stood when she'd come back into the room, but turned back to the screen when several players huddled on the mound, their words screened behind gloves, mitts and face masks.

"Interesting," she said calmly, placing the envelope on top of the *Coastland Times* on the coffee table when he failed to take it from her. If he left it behind again she would simply trash it. Let him find himself a relic from someone else's attic to use as bait.

"You read the letter?" He was still watching the game, but there was no mistaking who he was talking to.

"As much as I needed to."

"Then you understand what this is all about?"

"Oh, I understand. Don't let us keep you, Mr. Beckett, I'm sure you're a busy man."

Picking up on her skepticism, Beckett raised his dark eyebrows. In other words, go peddle your papers somewhere else, he interpreted, half amused, half irritated. If she'd understood only half of what she'd read, and been able to read just a fraction of what he'd given her, she'd done better than he had. Of course, he had the advantage of knowing what it was all about. The legend had been handed down in his family for generations. Once upon a time, someone named Beckett had cheated or stolen a sum of money from someone named Chandler. His mission was to make restitution so that the remaining Becketts could quit fighting their collective guilty conscience and concentrate on more important matters. Such as dealing with strokes, broken bones, Alzheimer's and emphysema.

The old man was watching them curiously instead of the action on the small-screen TV. Beckett would just as soon not have to try and explain over two sports announcers and a mob of cheering fans. "Look, could we go somewhere quiet where we can talk?"

"We've talked. I've read your papers, and I'm not interested." As if to prove it, she crossed her arms.

His stomach growled, protesting its emptiness.

Dammit, he needed to wind up this business and get back to his own life. He made the mistake of reaching out to lead her into the hall. The brief brush of his fingers on her arm created a force field powerful enough to set off mental alarms. If the startled look on her face was anything to go by, she'd felt it, too. Jerking her arm free, she led the way to the front door, held it open and stood at attention, waiting for him to leave.

Reaching past her, he closed the screen door. "Mosquitoes," he reminded her.

"Will you please just go?" Crossed arms again. The lady was at full battle stations. "Whatever it is you're doing, you're not doing it with me."

Oh, but lady, I'd like to. The thought came out of nowhere, catching him off guard. And dammit, he didn't need that particular distraction. He made it a policy never to mix sex with business.

"I'm not interested," she said flatly.

"You're not interested in ten thousand dollars?"

Her jaw fell, revealing a tiny chip in an otherwise perfect set of china-white teeth. Beckett found the small imperfection immensely satisfying for reasons he didn't care to explore. He was growing a bit irritated by her refusal to hear him out.

"No. Absolutely not. I told you, I don't play that kind of game."

"You think this is some kind of *game?*"

Her eyes flashed. "Isn't it?"

"No, ma'am, it is not!" He'd figured he'd be in, out and gone by now. Game or not, the lady wasn't playing by the rules, which made him feel better about leaving the envelope containing the money with the old man while she was in another room going over the documents. "This belongs to Ms. Edwards," he'd said to Uncle Fred.

"She goes by Chandler now. Maiden name. Don't want nothing to do with that rascal she married."

Beckett could understand why, if the police reports and press coverage had been accurate. "Would you mind giving her this after I've left? She'll know what it's for."

The old farmer had looked as if he'd like to know more, but just then, Chipper had hit a two-run homer. Then Queen Eliza had stalked into the room and tried to hand off the papers.

Now she did it again. He'd given the money to the old man, who had absently stashed the envelope under a half-empty potato chip bag. The papers had been left in plain sight. "Here, take these with you." She said. "Don't trip over that big oak root on your way out. It's buckled some of the flagstones."

Beckett stared her down. He was tempted to—

No, he wasn't. The only reason his glands were in an uproar was because he hadn't had a decent meal since he'd left his parents' home before daybreak that morning. Just because the woman was attractive didn't mean he'd lost his lost his mildewed mind—it only meant he hadn't lost his powers of observation.

He left, nearly tripping on the gator-size root. He quickly strode out to his rental, rationalizing that while he might not have a signed receipt, at least he had a witness. Tomorrow, on his way to the airport, he'd stop by and get the old man's signature on a statement saying that Ms. Chandler-Edwards had received the money. He'd be a fool not to. No telling how many heirs might come crawling out of the woodwork once word spread that someone was making reparations by paying off a generations-old debt.

In a certain fourth-floor apartment in South Dallas, Charles "Cammy" Camshaw hunched over a table, munching French fries and concentrating on the list he was making. "Look, we know for sure where she's at now. It's been a week and the letter hasn't come back, right? And it was her that answered the phone?"

"I don't know, Cammy, she was always real nice to me. I mean, like, what if we go to all this trouble for nothing? Driving all that way costs money, and like, we'll have to eat and sleep and all."

"I got it covered. We can write it off on our income taxes once we're up and running."

"I don't know," the shapely, freckle-faced blonde said again. She was sitting on the foot of the bed in a fourth-floor, two-room apartment painting her toenails a deep metallic blue. "You're so sure this is gonna work, but me, I'm not so sure. I mean, the police cleared her and all."

"Hey, that's what makes this so great. Can't you just see it? Cops clear suspect. Security guard—make that private investigator Charles Camshaw—digs deeper and solves the crime of the year."

"Huh. I wouldn't hardly call it that. He stole a whole bunch of stuff, but they caught him. Anyway, the guy was creepy, always smiling when people were looking and trying to cop a feel whenever his wife went out. But she was okay. I mean, she gave me stuff and all. She didn't act all stuck-up like some women I worked for."

"Yeah, well, once we get our business off the ground, you won't have to go nosing up to no society types. It'll be you and me, babe. Camshaw and Camshaw, Private Investigations at Bargain Rates. How's that grab ya?"

Patty Ann capped the bottle and wiggled her toes. "What if it's a bust? She sold off all her stuff—pictures and jewelry and some old furniture. Even her designer gowns. I was there when the lawyer showed up and she gave him the money so he could pay back what her husband stole. That don't strike me as being so bad."

"Hey, we're not going to do anything to hurt her, but you said yourself she was a smart lady. The way I see it, a smart lady would stash enough away until the stink blew over, then move to a brand-new location and start over, right? So she had a bunch of stuff and sold some of it—that was for show."

"You don't know that."

"Trust me, honey, in my business, you get to know how far people will go to survive. Now, I'm not saying she's done anything wrong, I'm just saying she's got plenty stashed away, waiting for things to cool down. You don't think folks might like to know where their money is?''

"They weren't even living together when he got caught. He was staying at a hotel, and she'd just rented this cheesy apartment—I helped her move, even after she told me she wouldn't be able to afford me no more.''

"I still say she was in on it. Maybe not all the way, but she had to know something. Way I see it, she copped a plea, and they let her off easy.''

"That's not what the papers said.''

"Don't trust everything you read in the papers. They can be bought off just like everybody else. Look, she's living it up out there on the beach, right?''

"It didn't look like a beach on the map.''

"Close enough. We've got her spooked now, so once we turn up she'll break and then we can get us a story and sell it to the highest bidder. I'm thinking *National Enquirer*, but I'll settle for the *Star*.''

"I guess,'' Patty Ann said doubtfully. "I'm startin' to wish I hadn't stole her address book. It makes me feel kind of…I don't know. Bad, I guess.''

"I know, babe. But look at it this way—she had her big chance. She blew it. That's tough, but hey, that's the breaks. Now it's our turn. Once we get the goods on her, we write our own story. If she's dirty, we go to the cops. If she's really innocent like you say, we go to the papers with a story about how this society woman is repenting her sins, living in the sticks and all. Papers pay big money for human-interest stuff, and the good part is, either way, we get our name out there. First thing you know we'll be going on all the talk shows, telling about how we tracked her down using no more than an address book, a few phone calls and a first-class stamp. That's real brainpower. Best kind of publicity in the world. Hey, we might even write a book.''

"Ha! Now I know you're crazy."

"Look, all I'm asking is, trust me on this. Either way it turns out, we get enough publicity to launch our business, and like they say in the movies, the rest is history.''

Patty Ann Garrett, currently employed by an old cow who called her Betty Jean half the time, idly scratched the back of her ankle with a freshly polished toenail. It was one thing to be in love with a brilliant, ambitious man. It was another thing to try and keep up with the way his mind worked. What if he thought she was too dumb and started looking around for another partner? She loved him, she really did. She'd loved him ever since they were in high school together.

"I guess it won't hurt to show up, like we just happened to be in the neighborhood and all.''

"I promise, we'll just show up accidental-like and talk to her.''

"Won't she wonder how we knew where she was?''

"I'll figure out something on the way. But listen, six years as a security guard is five years too much. The uniform's okay, but the pay's rotten and the benefits are worse. I been planning this thing for years, just waiting for the right opportunity to connect—something that'll get me some free publicity. You're my connection, babe. I won't forget it. From now on, we've got it made.''

It was too early to go to bed. Liza knew she'd never be able to fall asleep. Wouldn't be able to concentrate on the book she'd thought was so wonderful just yesterday, either. The writer was clever—she had a great ear for dialogue, but the hero was only in his twenties and had baby-blue eyes and boyish dimples. In Liza's opinion men didn't even begin to ripen until they were in their midthirties.

L. J. Beckett was probably nearing forty, maybe even a year or so on the other side. If he had a dimple, it was in a place that didn't show. Which brought on a whole new line of thought, one that was strictly off-limits.

"What's the score now?" she asked, dropping into the vacant chair, shucking off her clogs and sighing.

"Tied at three, but our guys is red-hot tonight."

"Ever the optimist." She smiled fondly at the relative she had never met until little over a year ago. He had saved—well, if not her life, at least her sanity.

There hadn't been any more hang-up calls for more than a week now, and the single letter could have been a fluke. Probably one of those automated envelope stuffers that couldn't tell when the ink ran out on the printer.

Oh, sure. The hang-up calls were wrong numbers,

and the blank letter was a computer glitch. And L. J. Beckett was a friendly IRS agent, trying to find out if she had stashed away any unreported ill-gotten gains.

"Storm looks like it's headed this way. Too far out to tell yet."

"Lord, not a rainy Labor Day weekend, that would be awful for everybody's business."

"Feet don't hurt, leastways no more'n usual. Maybe she'll sheer off. Feller said to give you this." Without looking away from the screen, her uncle fished out an envelope and handed it over.

Liza stared at it as if it were a copperhead poised to strike. "Do you know what it is?"

"Said he owed you some money."

"He doesn't owe me a darned thing. I've never even met the man before today."

"Seen a lot of folks in my life. This one don't strike me as a fool or a crook. He says he owes you money, it's 'cause he does. Or thinks he does. Any rate, you might's well open it, long's he left it here."

Liza could tell her uncle was burning with curiosity. Another batter struck out, and he didn't even turn to watch. "All right, I'll open it, but that doesn't mean…" The bills fell out in her lap. Ten of them, each featuring a portrait of Grover Cleveland. Nausea clenched like a fist in her belly.

"Cash money, huh? Know what that means? Means we don't have to report it."

When she could catch her breath again, she said,

"Uncle Fred, stop joking. I can't take this money. The man's out of his mind."

"Who says I'm joking? I've not got many more miles left in me, but I wouldn't mind seeing me a ball game at Turner Field. Might even take in a race or two while we're down that way."

Liza stared down at the Federal Reserve notes scattered on her lap. Ten thousand dollars. Nobody owed her so much as a single dollar, much less ten thousand of them.

"I've got to find him and give it back. Did he say where he was going?"

"Back to the motel, I reckon. Not much else he could do around these parts."

"He's staying at the beach?" She didn't look forward to driving all the way to Kitty Hawk at this time of night, but if he got away, she would never be able to put an end to this stupid charade.

"Fin and Feather, right up the road. Asked me this morning if there was a place, and I told him it was clean as any and cheaper'n most."

Liza continued to stare down at the bills scattered across her lap. She was so tired she could cry. Why couldn't people just leave her alone? She hadn't done anything wrong. She might have been stupid for not realizing where James's money was coming from all those years, but she'd paid for her stupidity. Paid for it dearly.

"I'll be back in half an hour," she said, gathering up the thousand-dollar bills and cramming them back into the plain brown business-size envelope.

He was good. Oh, he was good, all right, but whatever he was up to, she wasn't falling for it. Even stupid people could learn from their mistakes.

Beckett wasn't too surprised when lights flashed across the window of his unit, which was one of only five. He'd parked off to one side to avoid a pothole. Whoever had just driven up—he'd lay odds it was Queen Eliza—didn't care about potholes. Ten-to-one she was steaming. Back stiff as a poker, fire blazing in those whiskey-brown eyes. Oh, yeah, she'd be something to see, all right. Move over, Old Faithful, get ready to see a real eruption.

He opened the door before she could knock. Grinning, he asked, "What took you so long?"

Stabbing him in the chest with the envelope, she said, "You can take your blasted money and—and shove it!" She stepped back, but he caught her arm.

"Whoa…hold on a minute, how do I know it's all here?"

Her eyes alone could be classified as lethal weapons. Tossing the envelope onto the table beside the remains of his take-out meal, he led her gently into the room, careful not to exert any undue pressure. He had a feeling she would bruise easily.

Had a feeling she could also inflict a few bruises of her own, given the opportunity.

"Look, I think you've got the wrong idea about me—about what this is all about."

"I don't think so." Her arms were crossed again. If she had any idea what it could do to a man's libido to see a pair of small, soft breasts under thin white cotton, squished together and propped up on a shelf of tanned forearms, she'd be running for cover instead of glaring at him that way.

"I guess the papers have spent too much time in various attics over the past century or so. Charleston's gone through a few major hurricanes over the years—what with leaky roofs, hungry bugs and fading ink, it's a wonder we were able to resurrect even that much. The thing is, the Beckett men—" He broke off, wondering how to explain it in the simplest terms.

"The Beckett men *what?*"

He tried a smile on her, then shrugged and said, "They have a tendency to procrastinate. Look, could we sit down? It'll take a few minutes, but I'll try to sum it up. My father is Coley Jefferson Beckett. You might've heard of him, he was a state senator for three terms."

"Not my problem."

"Fine. The thing is, he was supposed to have located any Chandler heirs and paid them off years ago, only he was too busy campaigning. Now he's suffering from emphysema, so it's pretty much out of the question. Dad's brother, my uncle Lance, might've done it. Trouble is, he's got his hands full at the moment with—well, that's beside the point. That leaves me and my cousin Carson, who's currently laid up with a few broken bones."

Her eyes had gradually grown round with disbelief, so he hurried to finish before she got up and walked out on him. "But now that PawPaw's had this stroke—"

"PawPaw?"

"My grandfather. At any rate, it was PawPaw who originally promised *his* father to find these people and make good on the old family debt, only he never got around to it. I told you the Beckett men were good at procrastinating."

Liza stared at him for a full count. "Am I supposed to understand all that gibberish?"

"Yeah, I know what you mean. It's pretty hard to keep score. I've got a genealogical chart in my brief-case, but it's yours, not mine."

Frowning, Liza nibbled on her lower lip. She was half tempted to believe him, if only because the whole mess sounded so utterly absurd that nobody in his right mind could make it up. The con artists she'd read about usually went for simpler setups. The more complicated the lies, the easier it was to trip over them.

Actually, James was the only con she'd known per-sonally. When his palatial house of cards first began to collapse, he claimed it was all a mistake. Liza had tried to believe him. She'd lived with the man for nearly eleven years, after all. And although he was far from perfect—far, *far* from perfect—she'd once loved him enough to marry him. The initial passion had quickly faded, but she'd never had an inkling of what kind of man he really was until shortly before the end.

He'd always been something of a charmer—it was

one thing she'd come to despise about him. Teasing her and calling her his trophy wife, he'd spend a fortune on her clothes and jewelry, far more than she would ever have spent on herself. In the early years, he'd taken her with him to entertain potential clients. But then he began going on trips without her, which suited her just fine. By the time she'd learned about his mistresses, their marriage had essentially been over. She'd been more sad than angry. At that point, James had moved to a hotel and she had started divorce proceedings.

And then things had started getting crazy. First the police—two men from something called the Financial Crimes Unit. Then James's lawyer, her own lawyer, and then the victims' lawyers and, finally, the IRS.

Months later, after James had been shot and killed and she'd done everything she knew how to make amends to the people he had cheated, she started reading about all the ways unscrupulous people could trick gullible ones out of everything they possessed. What hurt the most was the fact that James's victims had usually been people who had saved all their lives for a decent retirement. On being told that they could live in relative luxury rather than eke out an existence in some low-rent retirement community, some had borrowed even more money to buy into whatever it was her bastard of a husband had been peddling. Offshore oil leases that never existed. IPOs for nonexistent companies that were guaranteed to double in value within the first three months. Promissory notes…

Oh, yes. James George Edwards had been smooth, all right.

And so was this man. "Do you have any identification?"

He pulled out a worn ostrich-skin wallet. Flipping it open to reveal a driver's license, he handed it to her. "Pilot's license? Credit cards? You want to see my business card?"

Liza shoved it back at him, trying not to notice the shape of his mouth, the way it moved when he spoke. "Business cards are a dime a dozen," she said flatly. "Same goes for fake licenses. I suppose next you're going to tell me you're a card-carrying member of the Screen Actor's Guild, right?"

He did a slow double take. "Beg pardon?"

All right, so he reminded her of a cross between Mel Gibson and George Clooney. "Look, can we just let this whole thing drop? I'm tired. I've obviously interrupted your supper. I'm not interested in accepting money from a stranger, so why don't we just leave it—"

A soft buzzing sound had him reaching for a cell phone. "Yeah? What's up, you find out anything new about the other one?"

And then he frowned. Liza couldn't help but stare. Even frowning, the man was strikingly attractive. He might even be on the level—she supposed most con games were built on a logical, legitimate premise. The missing heir or heiress. The forgotten deposit box. Did she dare trust him enough to explore any further? It might be…interesting.

Stop it. Just stop it right now. And stop what you're thinking about, too. Good Lord, you don't even like sex.

"Thanks, Car. If I leave now I can make it to the airport in about an hour, give or take. Meanwhile, keep me posted on any further developments."

Liza rose, thinking to escape while he was distracted. Something in his expression held her there. "Is anything wrong?"

He looked up, blinking as though he'd forgotten she was in the room. "PawPaw just had another stroke, a big one this time. He's in the hospital."

Four

He was gone. Out of her life for good. So why, Liza wondered, did she feel this nagging sense of disappointment? She didn't want his money. Even if what he said was true—that, way back in the dark ages, someone in his family had cheated someone in hers— what difference did it make now? L. J. Beckett hadn't cheated Eliza Chandler. Might've tried to, but he'd picked the wrong victim this time.

Still, she wished she knew. It would be nice to be able to dismiss him as a crook. That way she wouldn't waste any time mooning about him. Not that she intended to. Moon about him, that was. So he was good-looking; she'd seen far better-looking men. James, with his almost-too-perfect features, his carefully gym-contoured body and his impeccable wardrobe, had looked like a cover model for a men's fash-ion magazine...and look how he'd turned out. She was beginning to believe that handsome men were not only vain but they also relied too often on their looks alone to get them through life.

Oh, yes, she had definitely learned her lesson. The fact that she'd had no trouble resisting a ruggedly handsome man with a wild tale about wanting to make her rich...that just proved it, didn't it?

Sure it did. So why didn't she feel relief instead of this nagging sense of having missed out on something special?

It wasn't the money she was thinking about. It was L. J. Beckett.

PawPaw—Elias Lancelot Beckett—gazed up at his two grandsons, marveling silently that he'd been born in the nineteenth century, lived through the entire twentieth century, and would die in the twenty-first. How many men's lives had covered a span of three centuries?

Unable to participate actively for the past few years, he'd still made a point of keeping up with what was happening in the world around him. And what was happening, he thought, was that history kept right on repeating itself, with the same old lessons having to be learned over and over. At least the soldiers no longer wore red coats with a white X marking the spot.

Of course, that had been a few years before even his time....

He'd been watching the news last night when he'd had that little dizzy spell. Whole body had gone numb on him. Couldn't move. Couldn't talk. No point in watching the news if you couldn't talk back. By the time they got him to the hospital, some of the feeling had come back to one arm. But now he couldn't even shake a fist for all the dratted tubes they had hooked up to his body. He could've told 'em, if he could've got his tongue to work right, that all the potions Florence Nightingale and her friends kept pumping into his frail old carcass weren't going to do one dagnab bit of good. What he needed was a stiff shot of good bourbon.

Pain in the ass, that's what it was. Might's well die and be done with it, with all these wires and tubes and blinking black boxes hooked up to his body.

What are you two young nippers whispering about over there in the corner? You think just because I can't move, I don't know what's going on?

Eli saw the looks that passed between his two grandsons. He knew what they were thinking. Why'n hell don't this old buzzard pull the plug, head on upstairs and let us go home? He's taken up space down here long enough.

That tall, good-looking pair of fellers staring down at him like they wanted to cry but had forgotten how— they were his own begats, once removed. Big gray-headed boy looked just like him. Other one—Lance's boy—he had his mama's eyes. Blue as the fire off'n a stick o' lightwood. Young Lance had picked himself a real good-looking woman, that he had.

Elias Lancelot Beckett struggled internally to make wasted muscles respond to the command of his still-sharp brain. Silently, he shouted at his grandsons, telling them to quite wasting time hanging around here, to get on with doing what he should've done while he was still up and kicking.

Dagnab it, he'd promised his papa to find the man who'd delivered him, a man named Elias Chandler. Find him and pay back the money Papa owed him. Trouble was, he'd been having so much fun begetting and piling up worldly riches on top of what his papa had piled up before him that he'd put it off too long.

Of his five young'uns, only two had survived childhood. Whooping cough had taken the twins. Little Emaline had drowned in the creek. That had left Lance and poor Coley.

Lance couldn't do it. Coley, he couldn't do it, either. Nice enough fellow—smart for a politician, but sickly. It was up to these two, Lance's son Carson and Coley's son, Lancelot.

Good-looking boys, if he did say so. Both of 'em. Took after him in that respect. Likely had to beat the women off with a stick.

The years fell away, and Eli was once more a young man. Those were the days, oh my, yes. Smiling inwardly, although it never showed on his face, the old man closed his eyes.

"Should I call the nurse?" Carson whispered.

"He's sleeping. Mom says he sleeps most of the time. No pain involved—at least we can be thankful for that. Ever stop to think there could be a downside to the family longevity gene?''

"Tell you one thing—in case I live that long, I'm going to start practicing how to use my eyes the way PawPaw does. You ever get the feeling he's telling us to quit hanging around here and get on with paying off his debt?''

"It was actually his father's debt, the way I heard it.''

"Yeah...I guess.''

"Any luck yet? If you can get your woman to spread the wealth to the rest of her kinfolks, I'll ante up my share and we can wind this thing up PDQ.'' The men had agreed to put in ten thousand each of their own, without telling their grandfather. It wouldn't do PawPaw any good now to know that the stock he'd been supposed to deliver more than half a century ago was worthless—that while they'd all been fiddling away their time, Rome had burned.

The two men stepped outside in the hall, where they could speak above a whisper. Carson was hobbling around on crutches now. One of his arms was still in a sling, which made maneuvering tricky, but he got around pretty well for a guy who'd been targeted by a drug dealer armed with a two-ton truck. Beckett told himself it was a good thing his cousin was a fast healer, else he'd be ripe for a psychiatric ward by the time he finally shed the last of his fiberglass shell. Patience wasn't one of Car's virtues.

Nor his own, Beckett acknowledged.

"Mom's coming over this afternoon," he said. "Miss Dora will spell her for a couple of hours later on." He held the elevator door open, then waited until they were outside the hospital before bringing his cousin up-to-date. Standing in the shade of a big magnolia tree, he said, "You were asking if I'd located the Edwards woman? No trouble, I told you that on the phone. You want to know if I handed over the money? Yeah, I did that, too. Trouble is, she handed it right back."

"What do you mean, she handed it back? She crazy, or what?"

"Spooked, I guess. You read her record, at least what there was of it."

"Which wasn't all that much," Carson said thoughtfully. "Mostly, it covered the husband. If I remember correctly, no charges were ever brought against her."

"Yeah, well whatever happened, she's still gun-shy. I don't know—could be a guilty conscience for living high at the expense of all those poor suckers her husband conned. Maybe she's doing penance, living in a rundown house out in the middle of corn country, selling stuff in a roadside stand."

"Hey—whatever works. But she can use the money, right?"

"Oh, she could use the money, all right. The problem is getting her to accept it. I don't know if it's pride or what. I played it safe and gave her the papers to read first, figuring once she understood, we could wind things up. But, hell, you know the condition they were in, and when I tried to explain…."

Beckett shoved his sunglasses up on top of his head, sighed and mentally retraced his steps. "At least, I think I did. The old guy—the one she's living with? Baseball nut. There was a game going on with the volume turned up full blast, and to tell the truth, I'm not sure who said what, now that I think back. Once we got to my motel—"

"She went with you to your *motel?* Oh, brother."

"Hold on, it wasn't like that. I left the money with her uncle. Once she discovered it, she came after me, loaded for bear. Matter of fact, she was there in the room when you called last night."

"Okay, so you handed over the money. Then what? She gave it back? So where does that leave us?"

Beckett flexed his shoulders, trying to ease the stiffness in his back. Seemed as if he'd been sleeping in a different bed every night for the past year. Some nights he never even made it to bed. "Bottom line, I'll have to go back and hog-tie the lady long enough to make her listen, then stuff the money in her apron pocket and get out of Dodge—or whatever the name of the place is—before she can throw it back at me."

"Apron pocket? You trying to tell me the woman I saw on CNN wearing a hot-looking designer gown— the woman who owned a fancy house in Dallas and a condo in Vegas—she's wearing an *apron* these days? Man, that's taking penance pretty damned far."

Beckett nodded. He was dog tired from too many sleepless nights.

"Yeah, she wears an apron. But if you're thinking hausfrau, think again. Think like, diamond tiara wrapped up in brown paper sack. Any way you wrap it, it's still a diamond tiara."

"Classy, huh?"

"And then some." That was one way to describe her. Skinny women had never been a real big turn-on for him, but then, he'd never before met a woman like Eliza Chandler. "Funny thing, though—maybe I'm overcaffeinated, but I get this feeling there's something going on in her life that's got her spooked."

"So maybe she wasn't as clean as she was made out to be." Carson readjusted his crutch to a more comfortable position. "Maybe she copped a plea when her husband went down. According to my sources in Dallas, they didn't spend too much time together the last few years. He traveled a lot, usually with a female companion, but they put in joint appearances at a few fancy social functions. Art openings, charity bashes—things like that. Enough to get their names and faces in the social columns. According to one of the reports I read, she's not even on the books as a witness in New York, where a lot of this stuff went down."

"Yeah, well…that's their take. Big-city cops probably figured you bubbas down here wouldn't know what to do with the information if they handed it over, so why bother."

"Could be, Bucket…could be. Anyhow, this bubba

still has some work to do. I've got this physical therapist jerking me around three days a week. She looks like one of Charlie's Angels, but I'm pretty sure she was a drill sergeant in a former life.''

Beckett chuckled. ''You're the only guy I ever knew who flunked phys ed in high school.''

''Hey, it was boring, what can I say? I'm more the cerebral type. Look, how about asking your lady if she'll contact her cousin so I won't have to go through what you've been going through. This old body can't take too much more punishment.''

His lady. A vision of Eliza Chandler formed in Beckett's mind, complete with long, lean, calico-clad body, snapping light brown eyes and masses of auburn hair that refused to be confined. For a mouth that was clearly made for passion, hers could clamp shut quicker than any snapping turtle he'd ever taunted with a broom handle as a kid. ''You got it, but look—don't count on too much. First I've got to get her to sit still long enough to hear what it's all about. Evidently she's got her mind all made up that I'm some kind of creep trying to con her into playing games.''

''Now, why would she think that?'' Carson asked, all innocence.

''Dammit, not *that* kind of game!''

''Famous last words,'' Carson said with a smirk.

Liza threw her book across the room and asked herself why she'd ever wasted her money buying it in the first place. She knew the answer, of course. Because there was a baseball game almost every night, which meant that she could either watch with her uncle or go to her room and read. And because she didn't have a social life.

She'd declined several invitations—graciously, she hoped—from the women who supplied the stand, to join them at Wednesday night prayer meeting. By the end of the day, she was usually too tired to go out, anyway. Besides, she'd always been a reader. She had favorite authors she could rely on, knowing that no matter how frustrating her days were, she had a good, safe place to disappear for a few hours.

What she hadn't counted on was having the aggravating image of a man who might or might not be a crook come between her and the printed page. "Well, shoot," she muttered. Obviously, she'd been reading too many romances.

From the living room came the drone of the post-game analysis. Uncle Fred was snoring. She'd have to wake him up to go to bed, but that was all a part of the unspoken bargain they'd struck that day last spring when she'd shown up on his doorstep.

One of these days, she reminded herself, he wouldn't be here. She would miss him more than she would have thought possible only a year ago. The house would have to be sold, rotted eaves, sagging floors and all, and she'd have to move on. Again. She didn't want to think of it now, so, mostly, she didn't.

He was family, after all. The only family she had left except for a cousin she hadn't seen in years. And dammit, since she'd lost her address book, she didn't even have Kit's last address. She could write to the publisher, of course. Kit wrote children's books. She'd called over a year ago to say that her latest creation, *Claire the Loon*, was being optioned by a TV producer. Liza had been out, and Kit had left a message, but no clue as to how to get in touch with her. At the time, Liza had been putting the Dallas house up for sale and liquidating every possible asset. Evidently, Kit hadn't heard about the scandal. At least she hadn't mentioned it.

Liza bent to retrieve the book she'd flung across the room in disgust, mostly at herself for not being able to concentrate. She reached behind the door for her nightgown just as the phone rang in the kitchen.

It was too early for her creepy caller. On the other hand, it was too late for any of her suppliers. Uncle Fred's friends usually called during the day.

She reached for the phone on the fourth ring, then waited until the fifth to lift the receiver. "Hello?"

"Eliza?"

Air left her lungs in a whoosh. She felt behind her for a chair. "What do you want?"

"Would you please just set aside your suspicions and think about what I said? Ask your uncle if he knows anything about your family's history." Before she could respond, he said, "But I guess he's the wrong side, isn't he? He's your mother's brother, not your father's."

She hooked a chair with her foot and sat, willing her heart to slow down. "Actually, he's my maternal grandfather's brother, but that's none of your business." The silence lasted for three beats. Then, in a quieter tone, she said, "How about your grandfather, uh, PawPaw? Is he all right?"

"Thanks. Yeah, he's still hanging in there. Waiting for you to come to your senses and let me square things so he can die in peace."

She took instant offense, as if his grandfather's health were somehow dependent on her. "You're waiting for him to die? What kind of creep are you, anyway?"

Too tired to try to justify himself, Beckett cut her off. "Eliza, PawPaw's over a hundred years old. We're not quite sure how old he really is, but I don't think he'll be around too much longer. And, yeah, before you ask, I'm sorry. I'll miss him—we all will. Now, how about it, can we talk again? This time will you just listen while I explain and then take the damned money?"

"I'll think about it," she said after a long pause. Great. She'd think about it. "Fine. You do that."

Beckett decided to hold back on asking about her cousin Kathryn and any other cousins they hadn't been able to confirm until he'd solidified his position. After that, with any luck, he would be able to concentrate on business long enough to meet with a couple of ship owners in Newport News, maybe another one in Morehead City, and get back to Charleston in time to help deal with whatever came next, be it a nursing home or a funeral home.

God, he was tired.

Had he or had he not told her to expect him to show up in the next day or so?

Dammit, PawPaw, hang in there. I'm not ready yet to let you go!

After hanging up the phone, he sat in the semi-darkness of the east room of the elegant old house where the distinguished old man had once read him stories about Blackbeard's exploits off the Carolinas. Oddly enough, he could easily picture Eliza here in the same room, maybe arranging flowers or talking over the day's events with his parents, his friends.

The room no longer smelled of cigar and pipe tobacco, but of leather, wood polish and the eucalyptus oil his mother used to refresh her bowls of potpourri. It was a familiar smell, one he hadn't realized he'd missed until lately. Lavender in the linen closet, cedar in the coat closet, eucalyptus in the potpourri. Funny the way different scents could arouse different emotions, different memories. A whiff of cinnamon always made him homesick, no matter where he happened to be. His mother's cinnamon-raisin bread, fresh from the oven...

Rebecca Jones Beckett was a terrific cook. She and Miss Dora, the housekeeper, fought for kitchen dominance. Miss Dora usually won because of his mother's many social and charitable obligations.

Now she was spending most of her time at the hospital, taking benne seed wafers or whiskey cookies to the nurses, driving his father and his breathing apparatus back and forth and helping his uncle Lance interview companions for his aunt Kate, who was in the early stages of Alzheimer's.

Close family ties, Beckett thought with a deepened sense of his own mortality, were both a blessing and a burden. He couldn't imagine being without them. All the same, in these uncertain times he couldn't imagine a man's deliberately taking on the responsibility of a wife and kids. Not that there had ever been any guarantees.

Unlike premature graying, the commitment gene was one that had skipped his generation. Carson showed no more inclination to settle down than he did. Which probably meant the end of this particular branch of Becketts, he admitted with an unexpected shaft of regret. His mother would be disappointed. Already was, for that matter. She'd had her grandkids' names picked out and waiting for years.

Idly he wondered if it was family feeling alone that had brought Eliza Chandler from the high-rent district of a big Western city to the boondocks of rural North Carolina. Could be she was trying to outdistance her past, if she'd been a part of her husband's scams after all. Maybe she'd skated clear by using her looks and that touch-me-not attitude she projected so well. Wouldn't be the first time something like that had happened. On the other hand, she might simply have come to the rescue of an elderly relative.

He yawned, stretched and thought about replacing the mattress in his old bedroom with a king-size model. But that would mean getting rid of the old mahogany sleigh bed, and his mother would be unhappy. He'd sleep on the carriage-house floor before he'd add to her woes.

Not that he'd spent all that much time here over the past few years, anyway. If he ever did decide to move his headquarters from Delaware to Charleston, he would definitely need to get a place of his own, else his mother would be running his business instead of just trying to run his life. For all he loved her more than anyone in the world, Becky Beckett was one managing woman. The proverbial steel magnolia.

Five

It was two days later when Beckett pulled into the Grants' driveway. Queen Eliza's modest chariot was parked close to the house. Beyond that, between the house and a half-grown holly tree, what appeared to be an old Packard was permanently enshrined on four cement blocks. The fact that he even recognized the make made him feel older than his thirty-nine and a quarter years.

"Must be the life I lead," he muttered as he skirted a ladder propped against the roof, dodged a pot of pink and purple flowers and knocked on the screen door.

Funny, he mused as he waited for her to answer the door, the way the dilapidated old house looked so familiar. He'd been here, what? Twice? Even that crazy old fruit-and-vegetable stand out front, with its homemade counters and bins and its rusted tin roof, looked welcoming. He couldn't say much for her security system—a flimsy wraparound wall made of hinged lattice panels with a single padlock. But then, maybe fresh produce wasn't that much of a draw to shoplifters.

Beckett heard her muttering from somewhere inside the house. He'd tried unsuccessfully to call from New Bern and again from Elizabeth City. She needed an answering machine, if her old rotary dial phone could be retrofitted to support such an accessory.

"Ready or not, here I come," he muttered. He had a twinge in the small of his back from too many hours of driving and he was working on a pressure headache. Both complaints fell off the radar screen the minute he saw her.

What *was* it about this particular woman that riveted the attention of every male cell in his body? She was beautiful, sure, but he'd seen beautiful women before. Feature by feature, there was nothing particularly outstanding about her. Yet, even in the middle of a family crisis, he couldn't seem to pry her from his mind.

Which was plain crazy. Because despite the hasty research into her background and a few nonproductive conversations, he scarcely knew the woman.

She greeted him with a dry "I might've known." But then, he could hardly expect her to welcome him with open arms. He tried to picture her welcoming her late ex-spouse at the end of a workday. *Hello, honey, how was your day? Rip off any more senior citizens?*

Somehow, it didn't ring true.

She'd screwed her hair into a shaggy knot and anchored it with that tortoiseshell gadget again. She was barefoot, wearing pants that were a few inches too short—or maybe they were meant to show off her world-class calves. No makeup. Wouldn't want anyone to get the wrong idea, now would we? He wondered if she realized how sexy she looked with her naked mouth looking rebellious and just a little bit pouty.

"Am I interrupting a ball game?" he asked when she opened the screen to let him inside. Did it reluctantly, he noted with something akin to amusement. She wasn't going to give an inch, oh, no.

"The game was this afternoon."

"Right. I actually forgot this was a holiday weekend until I got out on the highway. Is your uncle…?" Raising a questioning brow, he nodded to the living room.

"Gone to bed. His arthritis bothers him when the weather forecast calls for rain—sometimes even when it doesn't."

"Old bones are a better barometer than any computer model NOAA uses, at least that's what PawPaw says."

Liza led him into the living room. It was smaller than his boyhood bedroom back in Charleston, its furnishings undistinguished—a few of them downright ugly—but it was a comfortable room. A small pile of orange peelings and a scattered newspaper indicated what she'd been doing when he'd arrived. He waited until she took her seat before settling onto the faux leather recliner.

"Would you like to have another go at the documents, such as they are, or would you rather I just cut to the chase and tell you what I know about how it all started?"

"Tonight?"

"I'm here. You're here." Granted, it was later than he'd planned. What with the way both clock and calendar had lost all meaning during the process of traveling between Delaware and Dublin, his parents' home and the hospital, then back and forth to this place, he hadn't realized until after he'd left Charleston what day of the week it was, much less that it was the start of Labor Day weekend. Once he'd hit the highway, traffic had been pretty much bumper-to-bumper in both directions.

"I'm listening," she said.

Yeah, sure you are, he thought. Her arms weren't crossed over her breasts yet, but that didn't mean she'd lowered the drawbridge. "There's really not much to tell. You looked over the packet. I've already given you a rough outline—at least, as much as I know about it. Evidently, our great-grandfathers were in business together around the turn of the century. Some kind of investment business, I believe."

The first shield snapped into place: she crossed her arms. He waited for her to comment, and when she didn't he went on. "I don't know what went wrong, but sometime after they split up, mine evidently got to worrying about some kind of debt he owed yours. Before he died, he asked his son—that's PawPaw—to make good on it. Incidentally, that's where the letter and the stock certificates came from.''

"Stock certificates," she repeated.

"Well, yeah...you saw it. Stuff's worthless now. I had it checked out with a broker. It might've had some value back in PawPaw's day—enough to cover whatever my family owed yours, at any rate. Now it's worth whatever a collector might offer. My guess—not even pennies on the dollar. It's yours if you want it, but to settle the debt, the Becketts—''

"Wait a minute, back up. If your—if the stock's worthless, where did the ten thousand dollars come from?''

Beckett frowned at a framed photograph on the mantel above the boarded-up fireplace. He could just make out a couple standing in front of a field of corn that was taller than they were. "Well, you see—''

"Just tell me the truth, that's all I ask. Because, quite frankly, when some stranger tracks me down and offers to give me something I've neither earned nor want, alarm bells start going off.''

"Right. Sure. I mean, I can understand that." *Under the circumstances* was implied. He was tactful enough not to mention it aloud. "But this is on the level. It started out with some old stock and a few promissory notes, but—'' Oops. Hadn't Car said that one of the charges the Financial Crimes Unit had nailed her husband on was selling fake promissory notes? "What I mean is—"

"What you meant was that since my husband was a crook, I must be one, too. Either that or incredibly naive. That I'll grant, but did you actually expect me to grab the bait and not even bother looking for a hook?" Patches of color bloomed on both her cheeks. "Or wait—I get it now. This is one of those pyramid schemes, isn't it? You hook me, then I'm supposed to talk all my friends into buying your worthless stock or notes or whatever, right? I'm supposed to get a big commission for every sucker I bring in. They drag in their friends, and they're promised commissions, too, only the commissions never happen. If that's the way it works, I already know the routine, so thanks but no thanks."

In other words, been there, read the book, bought the T-shirt. Beckett couldn't much blame her for being skittish, but dammit! "Look, I know what you must be thinking and I'm sorry, but I'm not your husband. This is on the level." He'd made the mistake of activating the recliner when he first sat down. Now he clicked the leg rest back into place, sat up and glared at her. "If you'd just listen to what I'm saying and stop—"

"I listened."

"—stop interrupting, maybe we could wind things up here and I could get on with my own business."

"Oh? You mean this isn't your real business?"

He looked at her.

"Would you like some coffee?" Her smile was utterly guileless.

"That's it. Try to throw me off balance so I'll forget where I was. Coffee? Yes, thank you very much, I would like a cup of coffee! Black, no sugar." And no arsenic, please.

That smile of hers would have one-upped the *Mona Lisa*, chipped front tooth and all. "Black, no sugar," she repeated. "Right. Now, why am I not surprised?"

She left, and a few moments later he got up and stalked after her. If she had any thought of slipping out through the back door, she was in for a surprise. It wasn't that he didn't trust her; surprisingly enough, he did. But Beckett had no intention of letting her off the hook, now that he was so close to winding things up. He had a feeling PawPaw might not be around much longer, and if he could do this one thing to put his mind at rest he would damned well do it. Even if he had to hold her down and force her to accept the money.

Five minutes—make that ten. Five for a cup of whatever brew she was concocting, five more to wind up this crazy business. Then he'd be on his way.

She hadn't escaped out the back door, after all. With a mutinous look on her face, she was measuring coffee, spilling almost as much as she poured into the filter basket.

"What's with the ladder I saw propped up against the roof? Getting ready to put up a bigger sign?" Two could play the game of diversion.

"Hardly. Roof rot. A section of gutter fell off this

morning, and Uncle Fred wanted to know if the roof was going to cave in.''

"Is it?" Leaning against a counter, he crossed his legs at the ankles. God, he was tired.

"Probably. Sooner or later. Nothing lasts forever."

"I'm surprised you could find anyone to check it out on a holiday weekend." Absently, he reached for a peach from the bowl on the kitchen table. Miss Dora always kept a fruit bowl filled in the kitchen of his mother's house. She used to swat his hand whenever he reached for a cookie before meals, but she never minded his sneaking fruit.

Now, without even thinking, he took out his handkerchief and rubbed the fuzz off before biting into the soft, ripe fruit.

"You might try washing it first."

"Sorry. What you mean is, I might try asking first."

"That, too," she said dryly, setting the coffee to brew. With any luck, he told himself, they'd have wound up their business by the time it was done. He could gulp and run. He needed the caffeine.

Wrong. Caffeine was the last thing he needed. He'd refueled his nervous system at every pit stop along the way. Maybe what he was looking for was an excuse to prolong his exposure to this maddening woman until he could figure out what it was about her that kept drawing him back here. He had an unsettling feeling it was no longer entirely PawPaw's unfinished business.

"What's the word on the gutter—eaves, whatever?'' If he could keep her off guard, maybe he could sneak in with a flank attack.

"I told you I don't know yet. I got out the ladder and set it up first thing this morning, but so far I haven't had a minute all day to go up and look."

God, she was something else. Up close, her skin was even more remarkable. Pale to the point of translucency. She smelled like soap and oranges. Probably rushed off her feet all day selling her cabbages and peaches and whatnot. On her, even exhaustion looked good. "You know, you really should hire some help. Has it occurred to you that while you're busy trying to operate that antique gizmo of yours, a lot of stuff probably walks out without stopping by the checkout counter first? Not all the pirates are on the high seas."

"You know, you really should mind your own business." She threw his words back at him. "Has it occurred to you that if I could afford to hire help, I'd have done it long before now? And for your information, I know—better than most, probably—that not all the pirates are on the high seas." She speared him with a look from her clear, whiskey-colored eyes.

"Ouch," he said softly. "Eliza, I'm sorry. I didn't mean anything personal, I was just making an observation."

He expected her to tell him to take his observations and hit the road. Wouldn't much blame her if she did. Instead, she did the last thing he'd ever have expected. "Have you eaten supper yet?"

Like a bear coming out of hibernation, his stomach growled. Well, hell. "Not yet. I was hoping to wind things up early enough to head back to Charleston tonight. Figured I'd get something to eat on the road.''

''You shouldn't drive when you're this tired.'' It was a quarter past nine.

''I'll need to go back at least as far as Elizabeth City to find a vacancy. The place where I stayed last time I was in this area is booked up, all five units. I called ahead once I saw all the traffic and realized what was going on.''

She got out a frying pan. Beckett bit into the peach, afraid to say more for fear of rocking the boat. Obviously exhausted, she was moving like a sleepwalker, and hungry as he was, he'd almost rather see her go to bed than stand there and cook whatever she had in mind to cook.

His imagination, hyped by too much caffeine over the long day's drive, created moving images of her elegant body stepping out of those rumpled pants, pulling the chambray top over her head and reaching behind to unfasten her bra. Women's arms were a remarkable feat of engineering, the way they could reach back and then so far up. Men's arms were different—at least his were. But even as tired as he was, he'd have made it easy for her if she'd asked. Pulled her closer, supporting her while he reached around and unhooked her bra, then eased the straps off her shoulders, following them with his lips until—

''One egg or two? I'm scrambling.''

''Uh…two?'' *Wake up, man, you're dreaming!* ''I can make toast if you'll show me where—''

"Bread box." She pointed it out, then indicated the toaster before dropping three slices of bacon into a skillet. Dare he hope one of them was for him?

"About the ladder—Eliza, you shouldn't—"

"Most people call me Liza."

"Thanks…Liza. Some people call me Bucket, but I'd appreciate it if you didn't." That earned him a reluctant smile. "You mentioned setting up the ladder. You didn't do it yourself, did you?"

"You think I'd let Uncle Fred lift something that heavy? I'm perfectly capable of carrying and setting up a ladder, but thanks for your concern. We don't have butter—we use that healthy kind of margarine. Uncle Fred's cholesterol isn't anything to brag about."

"Neither is mine."

She was trying not to smile again, but the corners of her mouth were twitching. Her eyes were sparkling again, too, this time not with anger. "Funny, the things men find to brag about, isn't it? Uncle Fred brags that his blood pressure is lower than his doctor's." Small talk. He could handle that. "Of course, that doesn't keep him from getting all hot and bothered and yelling at the TV."

"Any particular targets?"

"Politicians and baseball teams who aren't the Braves."

Grinning, Beckett accepted a plate with a mound of golden eggs and two slices of bacon just as the coffeemaker uttered its last gurgle. He dropped a slice of toast onto each plate while Liza set out a jar of fig preserves. "He and PawPaw would hit it off. PawPaw used to watch the news every night just so he could trace the ancestry of every politician even mentioned. You'd be surprised at how many unmarried mothers had sons who grew up and went into politics. Excluding my own father, of course. I've seen the marriage records inside the family bible."

She actually laughed aloud. Beckett wondered if sleep deprivation had finally done him in. He'd never before realized what a turn-on a woman's laughter could be. He said, "Nobody ever took offense. I guess it was just PawPaw's way of blowing off steam once he got too old to do much else."

"He lives with you?"

"With my folks. Uncle Lance and Aunt Kate would have been glad to have him, but our house is bigger. Dad and I used to watch Mom and PawPaw going at it over some issue or another and place bets on who would win the argument."

"I wish I'd gotten to know my family that well," she said wistfully.

She picked up a slice of crisp bacon, and he admired her hands. They were long, slender and looked surprisingly capable. In fact, he admired them all the way up to her shoulders. And beyond.

"My mother died when I was eleven," she went on. "My father remarried less than a year later, and he and his new bride moved to New Mexico while I was in boarding school in Austin. I visited during vacations, but somehow—you know." She shrugged. "It just wasn't the same. It was her house, not my home. Daddy was more her husband than he was my father.''

It was a perfect opening to ask about her cousin, the only other Chandler heir they'd been able to find. He hoped to God her father hadn't started a second family out in New Mexico, because as far as Beckett was concerned, the buck stopped right here.

She rose and topped off their cups and he murmured his thanks. At the rate he was drinking the stuff, he wouldn't have to worry about finding a room tonight. What was that old poem about having "miles to go before I sleep" or words to that effect?

They ate silently and efficiently. They weren't the best scrambled eggs he'd ever tasted—Miss Dora put cheese and sour cream in hers—but they did the job. He could have eaten half a dozen slices of bacon.

"You wanted to explain something," she reminded him.

Back to business. Beckett rose, scraped off his plate. Seeing no sign of a dishwasher, he rinsed it, left it in the sink and sat down again. As long as she was in the mood to listen, he'd better start talking. "To start with, this is something that's carried over for—what, four generations now? Like I said, we Becketts are notorious procrastinators.''

"Oh, I don't know…you're here, aren't you?" Even when she was tired, her smile got to him. There was something about her….

Or maybe it was just that his resistance was low. Lack of sleep, worry about his father and PawPaw— throw in irregular hours and too much junk food on the road and it was no wonder his mind kept straying from the business at hand.

Nah, it was the woman. Something about her seemed to resonate in a way that was…disconcerting, to say the least. He had a feeling that if they hadn't met here and now, they'd have met some other time, some other place.

Which was downright spooky.

"You do understand, then? You're not still thinking this is some kind of a con?"

Bedraggled and visibly tired, she blotted her lips with the grace and finesse of a grand duchess. "Let's just say I'm willing to listen with an open mind and this time I'll try not to prejudge. I won't promise to take whatever it is you want to give me—the money, I mean. It's not mine, no matter how much your family wants to clear its conscience, but if you can make your case before I fall asleep, I promise to listen."

"Point taken. Liza, did it ever occur to you that you could simply accept the money and hand it over to your favorite charity? Or buy your uncle a new roof?"

"I haven't—" But before she could say more, the phone rang. And rang again. Beckett glanced at the old-fashioned instrument and waited for her to reach for it.

On the third ring, he said, "Aren't you going to get it?"

"It's probably a wrong number. I get a lot of those."

"Dammit, it might be for me!" Before common

sense could kick in to remind him that anyone calli... him would have called him on his cell phone, he snatched up the receiver. "Grant residence, Beckett speaking."

Silence. He heard what sounded like a muffled whisper somewhere in the background and the connection was broken. "What the hell?" he muttered, glaring at the receiver.

"I told you so."

"Yeah, you did. Probably a wrong number."

When she shrugged and looked away, he said, "Liza?" Reaching across the table, he covered her hands with his. Hers were ice-cold. "You want to tell me what's going on here?"

She shook her head dismissively. "Oh, you know—kids' games. Call someone in the middle of the night and then hang up." It was hardly the middle of the night, but he got the point. "I'll probably go out some morning and find the stand's been decorated with toilet tissue."

His thumb continued to stroke the back of her hand. "Have you reported it?"

She raked back her hair with her free hand, causing the tortoiseshell clip at the back of her head to lose its grip. A length of wavy, auburn hair fell across her shoulder. Steeling himself, Beckett resisted the urge to touch it.

"It's only happened four times," she went on. "This makes five. And who would I report it to? What could the sheriff do? I doubt if even the phone company could do anything about it. Besides, it's just a wrong number."

"Was it? Maybe not. Have you considered getting caller ID, or having your number changed?"

"It's not my phone, it's Uncle Fred's. Besides, I don't know if the phone company would even let me do it."

"Who knows your number here?"

She shrugged again, a subtle movement involving no more than the lift of one delicate shoulder. He'd seen mimes that were more expressive. "Nobody, I guess. Uncle Fred has a nephew-in-law who calls occasionally. He works on a boat—one of those big container ships, I think. I meant to let my maid know where to get in touch in case anything came up later, but in all the confusion of putting the house on the market and packing up and—and everything, I forgot."

"Can you think of anyone else?"

She shook her head.

He said, "Close friends? Not so close friends?"

Boyfriends? It had been over two years since her husband had been murdered. If she'd been celibate ever since, it was a hell of a waste.

"Actually, I was busy for several months before I left Dallas—I sort of lost touch with my friends there." She smiled, and he wanted to tell her that it was okay. That he understood. But he couldn't tell her that without disclosing how much he knew about her past. He wasn't ready to do that.

"If it's someone from the IRS," she said, making

Play the LUCKY Carnival Wheel Game...

GET YOUR 3 GIFTS FREE !

PLAY FOR FREE ! NO PURCHASE NECESSARY !

HOW TO PLAY

1. With a coin, carefully scratch off the 3 gold areas on your Lucky Carnival Wheel. By doing so you have qualified to receive everything revealed—2 FREE books and a surprise gift—ABSOLUTELY FREE!

2. Send back this card and you'll receive 2 brand-new Silhouette Desire® novels. These books have a cover price of $4.25 each in the U.S. and $4.99 each in Canada, but they are yours ABSOLUTELY FREE.

3. There's no catch! You're under no obligation to buy anything. We charge nothing—ZERO—for your first shipment. And you don't have to make any minimum number of purchases—not even one!

4. The fact is thousands of readers enjoy receiving books by mail from the Silhouette Reader Service™. They enjoy the convenience of home delivery...they like getting the best new novels at discount prices, BEFORE they're available in stores. and they love their *Heart to Heart* subscriber newsletter featuring author news, horoscopes, recipes, book reviews and much more!

5. We hope that after receiving your free books you'll want to remain a subscriber. But the choice is yours—to continue or cancel, any time at all! So why not take us up on our invitation with no risk of any kind. You'll be glad you did!

A surprise gift

FREE

We can't tell you what it is...but we're sure you'll like it! A

FREE GIFT!

just for playing LUCKY CARNIVAL WHEEL!

Visit us online at
www.eHarlequin.com

LUCKY Find Out Instantly The Gifts You Get Absolutely FREE!

Carnival Wheel

Scratch-off Game

scratch off
ALL 3
gold areas

YES!

I have scratched off the 3 Gold Areas above. Please send me the 2 FREE books and gift for which I qualify! I understand I am under no obligation to purchase any books, as explained on the back and on the opposite page.

326 SDL DNXA   225 SDL DNW4

FIRST NAME   LAST NAME

ADDRESS

APT.#   CITY

STATE/PROV.   ZIP/POSTAL CODE

The Silhouette Reader Service™—Here's how it works:

Accepting your 2 free books and gift places you under no obligation to buy anything. You may keep the books and gift and return the shipping statement marked "cancel." If you do not cancel, about a month later we'll send you 6 additional novels and bill you just $3.57 each in the U.S., or $4.24 each in Canada, plus 25¢ shipping & handling per book and applicable taxes if any.* That's the complete price and — compared to cover prices of $4.25 each in the U.S. and $4.99 each in Canada—it's quite a bargain! You may cancel at any time, but if you choose to continue, every month we'll send you 6 more books, which you may either purchase at the discount price or return to us and cancel your subscription.

*Terms and prices subject to change without notice. Sales tax applicable in N.Y. Canadian residents will be charged applicable provincial taxes and GST.

a feeble attempt to laugh, "then they're out of luck. My income is a joke. If it's one of Uncle Fred's friends from Bay View—that's a retirement home over on the river—they'd be calling during the day. So, you see, it has to be kids. School starts in a couple of days, though, so it'll probably stop."

"And if it doesn't?"

"If it doesn't…" She bit her lip and looked away. Did she have any idea how tempted he was to gather her into his arms, find the nearest bed and curl up with her for the next few hours? No talking. No sex, just sleep.

Although, all bets would be off once they woke up together, rested and refreshed.

Six

Patty Ann lay curled up on the bed, watching the Weather Channel. Cam was in the bathroom shaving. She'd been the one to insist on sleeping in a real bed instead of in the car, but he'd been quick to take advantage of the facilities.

All she wanted was to stop moving, to get finished with this half-baked scheme, and go back home. She was beginning to think it was a bad idea even though Cammy said it was their big chance to get some free publicity.

"They say it's turning more northwest," she yelled through the half-closed bathroom door. "They show this yellow shape on the Weather Channel that's supposed to be where it's going. Are we headed anywhere near a place called Outer Banks?"

"Close, but quit worrying, hon, those guys always guess wrong. Anyhow, the place we're going, it's not right on the ocean. All we'll see is a bunch of rain. Trust me, would I put you in any danger?"

Patty Ann closed her eyes and sighed. She did trust him, she really did. Trusted his heart, at least, because that was just as honest as the day was long. His judgment was something else. It wouldn't be the first time he'd taken hold of some brilliant idea and not bothered to work out all the kinks before barging into action.

"Keep thinking about Camshaw and Camshaw, Private Investigations at Bargain Prices," Cam called. "Hey, you want in here before I grab a shower?"

"Uh-uh, I'm going to sleep." She fumbled with the controls to tune out a noisy commercial. "Rambo Camshaw, Harebrained Ideas, Two For a Nickel," she muttered under her breath.

After a brief argument—brief because neither he nor Liza had the energy to do more—Beckett ended up spending the night on Fred Grant's sofa. Lumpy didn't begin to describe the cushions. Now he knew where Liza stored her stock of root vegetables.

Still, it was better than trying to drive after about forty hours of sleep deprivation. He'd left a message, letting Pete know where he was in case anything came up at the office. Not that he expected anything to crop up over a holiday weekend. His partner was good at dealing with rules, regulations and red tape—better than Beckett was, at any rate. Which was why he'd hired him. As a negotiator, the guy had all the skills of a disgruntled cottonmouth, but he was a wizard with paperwork.

Good thing he'd driven instead of flying this time, he thought the next morning, yawning. Looked like they might be in for some heavy-duty weather. Lying on his back, Beckett squinted up at the ceiling for several minutes, trying to focus on how much more he needed to explain before he handed over the money, got a signed receipt and headed back to Charleston. He made a mental note to check on the storm situation. The last thing he needed was to get caught in an evacuation situation. Everything up and down the Eastern Seaboard was subject to that, if Tropical Storm Greta took a notion to upgrade and move inshore.

He yawned again as his eyes gradually shifted to the front windows. When the view registered on his brain, he sat up abruptly, grabbed the small of his back and groaned, staring at a pair of women's shoes planted on the top visible rung of the ladder.

What in God's name was that crazy fool trying to do? Avoid confrontation by breaking her neck? That ladder was a homemade job, the rungs roughly eighteen inches apart. It hadn't been designed for a woman, even a long-stemmed woman like Liza.

Beckett had slept in his clothes, removing only his belt, his shoes and his socks. He had about a two-days' growth of beard on his face, and his back felt as if it were broken in at least three places.

And now he had to go drag a crazy woman down from a roof?

Yeah, now he had to do that.

Barefoot, he let himself out the front door, wondering how he could get her attention without startling her into losing her balance.

She was humming. Either that or she'd disturbed a nest of yellow jackets. With his luck, it would be the latter. "Liza?" he called softly, trying to sound as nonthreatening as possible when what he wanted to do was grab her, haul her down and shake some sense into her stubborn head.

She stopped humming.

"What are you doing up there? If the eaves are rotten that ladder could shift any minute. Dammit, woman, it's dangerous!"

"Shall I rent a helicopter to check out the roof? Sorry, my budget doesn't run to aerial inspections." She started down, first one foot then the other, feeling for the rungs while he held his breath and stared up at her long white thighs. She was wearing shorts today. Not the kind cut up to the creases, thank God. His heart couldn't have survived that.

"Easy, easy—just two more rungs," he cautioned, moving into position to catch her if she stumbled.

"Get out of the way, in case I fall. I don't want to mash you."

"Go ahead, mash me," he said with a shaky laugh. By the time she was one rung off the ground, his arms were around her. Breathless, she turned, placed her hands on his shoulder, and he lifted her down. "Judas

Priest, woman, don't do this to me. With PawPaw in the hospital, my dad hooked up to a breathing machine, my cousin in a cast and my favorite aunt forgetting where she lives, I don't need any more problems.''

"Well, it's going to rain and the roof leaks," she said, looking at him as if she thought he'd lost his mind. Funny thing, though…she didn't move out of his arms. Just went on staring up at him while his senses absorbed her soap-and-shampoo smell, the heat of her skin and the birdlike delicacy of her bones.

At six-one, 182 pounds, he was not a huge man by today's steroid standards, yet she felt fragile in comparison. For one fleeting moment, before other impulses kicked in, she reminded him of a stunned dove he'd once briefly held in his hands after it had flown into a window.

Reminded him, too, of just how long it had been since he'd made love to a woman. She was staring up at him, her eyes wide with…shock?

Yeah, well, he was feeling his share of that, too.

When it came to women, Beckett's record was less than impressive. A generous man might describe him as cautious. He'd come close to falling in love a couple of times, but since his first disastrous affair, he'd made it a policy to steer clear of anything resembling commitment. Bad case of Once Bitten, Twice Shy.

So far as he knew, bachelorhood didn't run in his family. Just the opposite, in fact. His parents had fallen in love on their first blind date, married three months later to the day and never looked back, as his mother made a point of reminding him each time she launched into one of her latent-grandmother talks. Even PawPaw, when he used to talk about his Emaline, would get a certain look in his eyes.

Oh, yeah, Beckett thought wryly. The marriage gene was one family trait that had passed him by.

Not that what he was feeling had anything to do with marriage.

He'd held the woman's hand, eaten her scrambled eggs and tried to give her some money. He'd gone a lot further than that with dozens of women.

During his second year at Clemson he'd been involved with an art teacher who was really into New Age stuff. Claimed she'd recognized him from a former life. At the time, he'd been more interested in sports than philosophy, which had pretty much ended that affair.

But maybe there was something to the karmic theory. Why else would a woman he barely knew affect him the way this one did? Lust, he could understand, but this feeling of...of something else, that was harder to explain.

Karma. Sure. Like maybe you ripped her off in a past life, and now you're trying to make amends.

He'd been standing there for what suddenly seemed like hours, holding her—staring at the way her mouth looked up close, full and gleaming with moisture after she'd run a nervous tongue over it once or twice.

It would've been nice if one of them had a functioning brain. What the hell did a man say at a time like this, when he was visibly aroused with no chance of doing anything about it?

She was wearing a thin cotton top again, and it was pretty obvious she wasn't wearing a bra underneath. Or if she was, it was no match for those nipples of hers. They were standing at attention. Which sure as hell didn't help his condition. Here it was, broad daylight; they were standing out in the front yard, and he had no more control over his urges than a teenager.

He was about to make some inane remark about the weather when she reached up, brushed the hair off the back of her neck and said, "I wish it would hurry up and rain, leaks or no leaks. We need some relief from this heat."

Lady, you don't know the half of it. "You're not worried about the storm?"

She frowned up at the sky, which had taken on a nacreous tint as the first wave of clouds moved in. "Not worried exactly. It's awful for business, of course. Mine and everyone else's if they call for an evacuation, but I don't think it'll come to that. Uncle Fred says it's going to veer offshore."

Liza willed her heart to slow down. She'd never been afraid of storms, anymore than she'd been afraid of heights. It was neither the storm nor the ladder that had her gasping for breath, trying to slow down a runaway pulse. If she had to fall, she'd rather fall off the roof than fall in love again. It would be far less painful.

The first time it had happened she'd been eleven years old. Kermit Bryant—she'd never forgotten his name—had edged his seat closer to hers, leaned over and sniffed loudly. He'd told her she smelled good. Thrilled and embarrassed, she'd blushed and scowled down at her paper. Then he told her she sure could run good for a girl. She'd been thinking of asking if he wanted half of her devil's food cupcake when she'd caught him copying answers off her test paper.

Tall and skinny, she'd never been wildly popular with the opposite sex, but she'd dated some in high school and college. The next time she'd fallen mindlessly in love, however, she'd been a sensible, mature and independent twenty-seven-year-old gallery assistant. They'd been introduced at a charity fund-raising concert and James Edwards had literally swept her off her feet when someone in front of her had spilled a drink. She'd known him all of five days before ending up in his bed.

God help her if she ever did anything so stupid again.

Now she caught herself staring at Beckett's bristly jaw and wondering if it would grow out as black as his eyebrows. Embarrassed, she blurted, "Do you want coffee before you go?"

Oh, God. She had all the savoir faire of a week-old gosling. His smile was so gentle she had to wonder if he'd read her mind.

"I've already put you to enough trouble."

His khakis were wrinkled, the tail of his black knit shirt hanging out; his hair was standing on end, he needed a shave and he was barefoot. And at this moment if he'd asked her to undress and follow him into the nearest bedroom, she wasn't entirely sure she'd say no. Even rumpled, there was something remarkably appealing about him. He smelled warm and clean and real, the way a man should smell. James had adored cologne and used it with a lavish hand.

Whatever it was with Lancelot Beckett that affected her the way it did, it was 100 percent natural. Pheromones. She hadn't a clue about their chemical components, but they were clearly potent. That much she did know.

"We're out of prunes again," came a disgruntled complaint from the doorway.

Liza closed her eyes, torn between laughter and tears. They went through this every morning. It took Uncle Fred awhile to assimilate new developments. At this particular moment, she could certainly empathize.

"They're in the cereal cabinet, Uncle Fred. I'll come show you."

"Young man here for breakfast? That's nice. Game starts at one. That new feller's pitching. Reminds me of Maddux in the old days."

"Thanks, but I can't stay," Beckett said. "As soon as I have a few words with Liza, I'll be on my way."

Already hurrying into the house, Liza glanced over her shoulder, "I can't talk now—I have to find Uncle Fred's prunes, and then I have to dress and get ready to open up in case any stragglers stop by." She paused long enough to say, "Look, do we really need to talk anymore? I think we've both said everything that needs saying."

"One thing I learned a long time ago—when it comes to negotiations, you're not finished until both sides agree that you're finished, even if it's only an agreement to disagree. So far we haven't even reached that point."

"Sure we have, don't you remember?"

"Look, I'll drop by later, all right? I've got a few calls to make—I might even run up to Newport News, but I'll be back this afternoon. Have dinner with me and we'll wind things up." He turned away before she could reject the invitation. Halfway to his car, he realized he'd forgotten his shoes, his belt, his wallet and cell phone.

Well, hell. Wincing at every other step, he avoided the buckled flagstone walk as he made his way back to the house.

"Forget something?" she said a little too cheerfully from the open doorway.

He glared at her. "Go ahead, gloat," he muttered under his breath.

"It's the holly leaves. They're almost as bad as cockleburs." She was grinning broadly by the time he reached the front steps. "I never would have taken you for a tenderfoot."

His dignity already in sad repair, he tried to glare at her, but ended up chuckling. "I'd forgotten how long it's been since I went barefoot."

Still smiling—he refused to call it smirking—she led the way past the living room where he'd left his personal effects. She nodded toward the bathroom and suggested he might want to wash up before he left.

Splashing cold water over his face and throat, Beckett considered telling her that there'd been a time when he could grind out a cigarette butt with his bare heel. Back in his reckless, hard-drinking, sports-fishing, womanizing days.

Aware that he was in danger of regressing, he combed his hair, examined his stubble and decided it could wait another few hours before reaching the itchy stage. By the time he returned to the kitchen, she had his breakfast on the table. The electric moment they'd shared out in the yard might never have happened.

Or maybe they hadn't shared anything at all— maybe he'd been the only one stunned by the unexpected current that passed between them when he'd lifted her down from the ladder. Sure, she'd been breathing hard. The pulse at the side of her throat had been fluttering like a captured wild bird. It could have been from exertion.

But dammit, exertion couldn't account for the fact that her nipples had been standing up like a pair of tiny thumbs poking through her soft cotton shirt. And it sure as hell wasn't the temperature, because today promised to be another steam bath. There was only one explanation: she'd been as aroused as he was.

Smiling, Beckett slipped into a chair and inhaled the fragrance of freshly brewed coffee. The kitchen was about a third of the size of his mother's kitchen back in Charleston, yet there were enough similarities to make him feel right at home. It was a…a family feeling, for lack of a better word.

Liza shoved the fig preserves across the table. Uncle Fred smacked his lips and said, "What did you say you did for a living, young man?"

He didn't recall saying, but maybe he had. "I sell insurance." It was the simplest way to put it. He sold security systems that could be installed on ships to help track them and alert the owners if one of them strayed off the charted course.

"Got anything that covers rotten roofs?"

"No, I'm afraid not." So then he had to add a little more, explaining the growing threat of piracy that had bankrupted more than a few small-ship owners. While the two men talked, Liza listened, her expression telling him she wasn't buying it. Not the whole package, at any rate. But then, she'd probably earned the right to be suspicious.

"Pirates? You're kidding, right?" They were sharing cleanup tasks while her uncle read the morning paper in the living room. Liza had gone out to open the stand and returned a few minutes later. When business was slow, she explained, she could keep an eye on it from the house. Today she'd be lucky to sell much of anything.

"Yeah, I know—it sounds crazy, but it happens more than most people think, if they think about it at all. Just like in the old days, it's usually a matter of profit. Occasionally it's desperation—a handful of poor thugs feel like they have nothing left to lose, so they hijack a ship, planning to sell the cargo to help feed their families. Mostly, though, it's a calculated risk. Like bank robbery, only on a slightly larger scale. My business is to cut the risks for ship owners and insurance companies as much as possible.''

"With what, armed guards?" She raked a few strands of hair from her brow, leaving a blob of soap-suds behind. Beckett turned her to face him, tilted her chin with one hand and blotted the suds with the dish towel.

Without releasing her, he said gruffly, "Mostly tracking. Monitored GPS systems. If a ship goes off course, certain steps are taken and then—"

He sighed. "Liza, I think I'm going to have to kiss you. Consider this fair warning."

She didn't move. If anything, her mouth softened, those full, naked lips parting on the whisper of a sigh.

One touch was all it took. What started out as a gentle exploration quickly escalated into a full-scale assault. His hands moved from her shoulders down her back, pressing her against him as he angled his face for better access. Scented heat seemed to rise and swirl around them. Her lips trembled and conformed to his as if they'd been made to fit together.

Beckett groaned. His tongue engaged hers in a dance as old as time. Tasting mostly of coffee, with a deeper, more personal note that affected him pro-foundly, she felt incredibly right in his arms. Almost familiar—as if they'd done this a thousand times be-fore, yet each time it happened it was a brand-new experience.

Man, you're losing it.

Then consider it lost, the last reasoning cell in his brain shot back. She couldn't have fitted him more perfectly if they'd been adjoining pieces of a puzzle, her pelvis nestled against his throbbing groin, her breasts flattened against his chest. It was like coming home. Forcing himself to hold back, he used the tip of his tongue to trace a line between her lips and her ear, nibbling little kisses along the way, grazing her with his teeth, then soothing her with his tongue.

She was trembling, her breath coming in irregular little gasps. Her fists were bunched in his shirt—he imagined them clasping him the same way.

Finally, painfully aroused, with no relief possible, he forced himself to begin easing away. He'd already put on his belt, but his shoes, wallet and cell phone were still in the next room, along with Uncle Fred.

From outside came the abrasive blare of a car horn. Liza groaned softly and buried her face in his throat. Beckett wanted nothing more at that moment than to back her up to the table, spread her legs and move between them. But it wasn't going to happen. Not now—probably never.

Sounding flustered and embarrassed, she said, "I'd better go out and—oh, shoot! I'm not even dressed." She was still wearing the shorts, clogs and faded shirt instead of her uniform of slacks and calico apron.

Beckett caught her when she would have slipped past him to dart into her bedroom. "Liza…don't." He wanted to tell her not to be embarrassed. He settled for, "Don't change, you look fine. Let me go out and see what they want. I'll hold 'em until you get whatever you need and get out there, okay?"

"My apron...the till," she said breathlessly.

And so he went outside, still barefoot, hoping his arousal would take care of itself before he had to discuss the price of turnips with a bunch of tourists.

Seven

"**I** want to go home." Patty Ann's face was pale under her freckles. Her conscience was bothering her. "Cammy, she hasn't done anything wrong. Maybe we shouldn't do this."

"Head still hurtin' you? Swallow another one of them pills." She'd had a headache earlier. "Honey, you said yourself she was smart. Now I ask you, would a rich lady that was smart give away everything she's got and walk off, not knowing where her next steak dinner was coming from? Trust me, in my line of work, you have to get to know people."

In his line of work, he had to know how to punch a clock, Patty Ann thought, and was instantly awash in guilt.

Absently, Cammy patted her on the knee. "Look,

the old man she's living with, he's not going to let her starve, right? He's got a house and all—probably some rich old coot—maybe he's kin, maybe not. But if she's as smart as you say she is, she'll stay put until she gets ready to make her next move.''

"I think he's her uncle. She said something once…" Patty Ann's voice trailed off as she thought of how well she'd been treated over the five and a half years she'd worked for Ms. Edwards. If she hadn't already hired herself another maid, maybe Cammy could find a job at this place they were going, and she could go back to work for Ms. Edwards, and they could forget all about starting a private investigating agency. Cammy had been studying for months, but he still had to get a license. And even as brilliant as he was, Patty Ann wasn't sure how good he was at taking tests. She would still love him. She always had, but in some ways men never did grow up.

"Listen, the letter didn't bounce. She's still there— you found that out when she answered the phone."

"Yeah, well a man answered once."

"Sure. The old guy. Look, hon, chances like this don't come along twice. 'Member that guy down in Atlanta when some creep set off a bomb at that Olympic place? He was a security guard, just like me. Once it was over, everybody in the country knew his name."

Patty Ann hauled off and whopped him on the shoulder, causing the old Chevy to veer toward the centerline. "Cam-my! Everybody thought he was a crook! We're not crooks!"

"Neither was he. See, that's what I'm getting at, babe. Publicity's the name of the game. You get it any old way you can."

He flashed her a quick grin, and Patty Ann was reminded all over again of why she loved this man. Most handsome guys were full of it, but Cammy had never been stuck on himself.

"Like I said, once you get enough publicity, people remember your name, but they forget where they heard it."

"Yeah, sure they do," Patty Ann grumbled half-heartedly. He was not only handsome, he was sweet and way smarter than people gave him credit for being. Sometimes she wished he wasn't so smart. Truth was, it didn't seem so smart to her to quit a good steady job to gamble on some crazy scheme that might even land them both in jail. For all she knew, calling somebody on the phone and then hanging up could be against the law. Cammy said it wasn't, but he hadn't graduated from his correspondence course yet. Maybe that was in one of the last lessons.

"Look, we'll stop off in the next town we come to and get something to eat, that'll make you feel better."

"Starting my period'll make me feel better," she mumbled.

"Jeez, you don't think you're pregnant, do you? Honey, I told you, we can't afford kids until we get our business up and running. I figger a couple of years ought to do it if we can get us some publicity. Then we start with a blast and the sky's the limit."

"Uh-huh." The Edwards case had been big in Texas, but maybe not anywhere else.

"Whatcha want for lunch, burgers and fries?"

"I don't want anything, I already told you. Maybe hot cocoa. Not the kind from a mix or a machine, either—the kind you make on the stove with cocoa and milk and all."

"Ba-abe, come on, we're in this together, remember? Another few hours, we ought to be in the neighborhood, then I'll spring for another motel room and we can shower and all before we show up at her place."

"I don't know…"

"Hey, maybe she'll invite us to stay. Ocean beach just a few miles away? Probably got a swimming pool and all?" Catching her skeptical look, he said, "No? Okay, but just keep saying it over in your mind… Camshaw and Camshaw, Private Investigations at Bargain Rates. Maybe something on the next line about discreet and all. Think about it, okay? I'm going to stop in the next town for food and gas."

Liza sprayed a whiff of her favorite fragrance. The bottle was practically empty, and once it was gone she would do without. If Beckett thought she was wearing it for him, then that was just too bad. She was wearing it for herself, along with one of the few decent outfits she'd kept when she'd sold practically her entire wardrobe. For a while she'd felt guilty about keeping back anything at all, but now she was glad she had. It helped to remind her, in case she was in danger of forgetting, that there was more to life than a produce stand, a house that was gradually sinking into the ground and a dear old man who was totally dependant on her to look after him.

"Just a few hours of my own, that's all I want," she told her mirror image as she arranged her hair in a softer style.

Liar.

She had just finished putting on her earrings—a pair of simple, inexpensive onyx studs, when Beckett arrived, his head and shoulders covered with a limp newspaper. "Hey, I hope you have a raincoat. It's really starting to come down."

She had a cheap plastic raincoat. No way was she going to wear that. Instead, she reached into the coat closet for her uncle's big umbrella. It was so old the black had turned green in streaks, but it didn't leak. Uncle Fred was watching an Andy Griffith rerun, waiting out a rain delay before the game could get started. He would stay up for hours if there was the slightest chance of resuming play.

Liza had cooked him a squash casserole with cheese and made apple pie for dessert.

Before coming to North Carolina she'd done very little cooking. They'd always had a live-in cook while she was growing up, and James had preferred eating out. Actually, he'd preferred being seen in all the best restaurants among all the best people, only his idea of best and Liza's had gradually diverged.

After seeing the way her uncle ate, mostly junk food and things that came out of a can, she had quickly learned her way around the kitchen. In fact, she might even write a cookbook one of these days—101 ways to use up leftover produce.

Beckett stepped inside, looked her over and whistled silently.

"Too much?" She shouldn't have dressed up, especially as it was starting to rain really hard. Now he'd think he had to take her somewhere special.

"Too much," he echoed admiringly, giving the words an altogether different meaning.

She looked in on her uncle to be sure his chair was tipped back so that he wouldn't topple out if he fell asleep. Gently she removed the remote from his hand so that he wouldn't drop it when he dozed off, and then touched him on the shoulder. "Uncle Fred, I'm leaving now."

"Wha—what's that? Who's this? Who let you in?"

"It's Liza, Uncle Fred. I told you, I'm going out for a little while, but I'll be back soon. You go on to bed whenever you're ready, I'll look in on you when I get back."

The old man smacked his mouth few times, mumbled something about possums and was snoring softly by the time she reached the front door. "I don't know if I should go or not. I feel guilty about leaving him, even for a few hours."

"How long had he lived here alone before you came?"

"You're right. I guess I'm trying to make myself

feel indispensable. He lived here alone for years before I arrived on the scene.''

Beckett took the umbrella from her, opened it on the porch and held it so that it covered them both as they passed by the ladder that was still propped against the eaves. ''Notice I didn't open the umbrella in the house, and we walked beside the ladder, not under it.''

She slanted him a quick smile that made even the soles of his feet tingle, ''Duly noted.''

To shield them both from the blowing rain, he had to wrap his free arm around her waist. Feeling her hip pressed against his as they hurried out to the car, he found himself almost regretting his impulsive dinner invitation. Liza in calico and wrinkled linen was enough to make a man forget his own name. Liza in a flowing black skirt with a silky shirt was enough to make him forget to breathe. He finally remembered, only to be sucker punched by the tantalizing whiff of some cool fragrance that mingled enticingly with her own subtle scent.

''You did something to your hair,'' he accused, steering her carefully over the uneven flagstones. It was looser than usual, a few wisps left to trail down her nape and over her temples. Tempting as the devil.

He hurried her out to where he'd parked his car, a few feet away from where the tin roof of the produce stand was being hammered noisily by the rain. Even for a guy who knew his way around most of the large port cities on three continents, it was surprising how quickly this particular wide spot in the road had come to feel so personal.

Beckett held the passenger door open, shielding her with the umbrella as she swung her long legs inside. If he got any wetter he'd be sending off steam.

Once inside, he started the car and backed out, unable to think of a single intelligent thing to say. Delayed adolescence overlapping premature senility. Hell of a thing.

"You probably know more about the restaurants around these parts than I do. Any recommendations?"

"Beckett, we can get something from a drive-in if you want to. I just needed to get away for a little while. You don't have to feel obliged to entertain me."

They were on a straight stretch of highway, which helped, because he found it impossible to devote his full attention to driving. "Look, let's get one thing straight. No, let's get several things straight. I came here with a purpose, we both know that—not that we ever reached an agreement, but at least you know why I tracked you down in the first place." He waited for a response.

Then, a direct man by nature, he figured he might as well lay his cards on the table. "What happened next was as big a surprise to me as it is to you. I don't know what to call it. I do know—at least I hope—that it's not entirely one-sided. You want to tell me I'm wrong?" he challenged.

Passing cars and the occasional neon sign only served to emphasize the premature darkness. Rain continued to fall, creating an odd sense of intimacy. By the time they reached the Currituck Sound Bridge on the way out to the beach area, traffic had noticeably increased. It was all headed inland, a steady stream of oncoming headlights.

"What was the name of that man?" she said.

"You mean Wrong Way Corrigan?" Beckett picked up on it immediately. For every three cars headed to the beach, at least a dozen were headed the other way. "Turn on the radio, see if you can find a weather broadcast. I have a feeling we're missing some information." Come to think of it, he'd stopped following the storm news once he'd got here. Too many other things on his mind.

She scanned past blurbs of music, past several commercials, and stopped on a news break. "...not expected to run for another term. Meanwhile, Greta is now a full-fledged hurricane. She's expected to strengthen by the time she reaches land. Hurricane warnings are posted for—" a burst of static interrupted "—South Carolina. If she stays on her present course—" More static. Before he could switch to an FM station, the cheerful voice came back. "...or possibly head inland. Stay tuned for the next update."

He turned the sound down. Neither of them spoke. As Beckett continued to drive, the only sound was the *slap-slap* of the windshield wipers and the rhythmic *bump-bump* of expansion joints as they crossed the long bridge. Nearing the beach, the unbroken line of oncoming headlights had Beckett swearing under his breath.

Suddenly he turned sharply, pulling into a visitors' center perched high on a dune. Parking so that they had a clear view of the intersection where north and south beach traffic merged to head inland, he switched off the engine and said quietly, "Well, hell."

For several moments the only sounds were the *tick-tick* of cooling metal, the steady drumming of rain and the occasional sound of screeching brakes and blaring horns. Even so, as evacuations went, it was surprisingly orderly.

"He said something about South Carolina. How far is your family from the coast?"

"Not right on the beach, but close enough to catch hell if it comes ashore anywhere in that area." Beckett shifted in his seat so that he faced her. "About the same distance as you and Fred are, but at least our roof doesn't leak. Dad replaced the whole thing after Hugo."

"Know what I think? I think we should just forget about this family debt business. If it's waited this long, another generation or so won't matter. Whatever Greta does, you need to be there for your family and I need to be there for Uncle Fred. In fact, I think we'd better head back and get started right now."

"Get started doing what?"

She appeared to consider the idea. He waited, aware of her warmth and the faint scent of a very good perfume. He didn't know what it was, but it lacked the shrill edge of some of the more modern scents. Just as Liza lacked the hard edge of too many women he'd met, including a few he'd been briefly involved with.

"Well, actually, I'm not sure. In Dallas we don't get too many hurricanes. Uncle Fred will know, though. At any rate, you don't need to waste any more time here. If you start back right now…" Her smile was a little too quick, a little too bright.

"I'll get bogged down in traffic. If this really is an official evacuation, every room within miles is going to be booked up. People who've rented cottages for a week aren't going to miss out on any more beach time than they have to."

"You can't drive all the way back to Charleston tonight."

"I don't intend to."

"But what about your family?"

"I'd say South Carolina's pretty much in the clear by now, if they're starting to evacuate this area." He turned to her then, both his features and hers illuminated by the security lights surrounding the sprawling rest area. "Liza, things aren't turning out the way I'd planned. Under the circumstances, I guess dinner at a restaurant is out. They're probably busy right now boarding up windows. So why don't we find a grocery store and stock up on the basics, then go back to Uncle Fred's, light a few hurricane candles for a festive touch, and open a few cans? What do you say, corned beef hash or roast beef hash? Fried up with onions and tomato sauce, they taste pretty much the same to me."

"You mean ketchup." She laughed.

Beckett thought, another woman would have whined about having her evening spoiled and sulked all the way home, but not Liza. Sitting there in a deserted parking lot in her silk finery, with her hair all soft and sexy, smelling like three hundred bucks an ounce, she was laughing.

You had to love a woman like that, you really did.

Oh, no. No way!

"Where's the nearest supermarket?" he asked gruffly, scowling as he started the engine and circled the dune to pause at the intersection. Better keep his hands occupied, else he might reach out to her. One touch and all bets would be off as to which way this evening would end up. He could tell by a certain uneven quality of her voice that he wasn't the only one affected by the unnatural tension.

"There's one a few miles ahead on the beach, and another one back in Grandy. We passed it on the way."

"I vote for Grandy. Here's hoping it's still open." After several minutes he got a green light and merged with the traffic flow. Thank God there were signal lights at the intersection or they'd have been stuck here for the duration. A couple of decades ago he might have welcomed the opportunity. But Liza wasn't the kind of woman you made it with in the back seat of a car.

The tension mounted even higher as they were forced to maintain the bumper-to-bumper pace. Liza found a classical music station. Sebelius helped. If he'd been alone, Beckett might've pulled over and waited it out. With Liza beside him, that wasn't an option. Patience, as he'd been reminded more than once recently, was not his strong suit.

They bought the last two loaves of bread on the shelves and one of the few remaining gallons of milk. Liza added an assortment of canned soups and cookies, while Beckett raided the meat counter.

"What if we lose power?" she asked, on seeing all the perishables in his basket.

"We cook it all and pig out."

"Who's this *we?* You're going back to Charleston, aren't you?"

"Depends," he said, not bothering to elaborate.

"Beckett, they're already evacuating the beaches. That means it's headed this way real soon."

"Not necessarily. A lot of people will clear out, even before an evacuation is called for."

"Yes, well…" Liza leaned forward, trying to see the now-familiar landmarks. Everything looked different at night. She could count on one hand the number of times she'd been out after dark. The rain only made it worse. Neon signs, taillights, the occasional streetlight, all reflected on wet pavement.

Slowing, Beckett made a right turn. "Here we are," he said.

Liza hadn't even realized they'd arrived. She felt a thread of resentment that her evening out had already ended, accepting the guilt that followed hard on its heels.

And then she noticed that all the lights in the house

were on. "Omigod," she whispered, and without waiting for the umbrella, she opened the door, slid down to the ground and started running.

Beckett was two steps behind her. He yelled for her to watch her step just as the heel of one of her flimsy sandals skidded on a wet stone. Arms flailing, she was trying to save herself when she tripped.

He was beside her in an instant, kneeling, touching…running his hands down her legs. "Jeez, don't move, okay? Let me—"

"I'm all right! Dammit, just give me a minute." His hands were getting tangled in her wet skirt as he felt to see if she'd broken any bones. She hadn't. She was fairly certain of that. All the same, when an adult fell, it wasn't quite the same as when a child took a tumble. "My hands and knees burn like the devil, but I'm all right," she said through clenched teeth. "Go see what's happened to Uncle Fred."

She was furious. What an utterly humiliating way to end her big evening, sprawled out in the pouring rain on her hands and knees. Or, rather, her knees and chest. Her hands had skidded out from under her when she'd tried to save herself. They hurt almost as much as her knees.

"I'm going to pick you up. If anything hurts, speak up."

Everything hurts, dammit! She thought it, but didn't say it. Walls of wind-driven rain flew at them as, ever so carefully, he eased her over onto her bottom and lifted her off the ground. "Okay so far?"

"I can walk, just give me a minute," she growled,

making no attempt to free herself. Aside from hurting, she was badly shaken. "What I need to know is why all the lights in the house are on."

With her head tucked up under his chin, her long legs dangling, Beckett carried her carefully up the front steps and onto the wet porch. The door opened almost immediately. Fred Grant said calmly, "Saw the lights turn in. Thought it was you." He was standing there in his best bib overalls, his blue-and-white striped Sunday shirt and his Braves baseball cap. On the floor beside him was Liza's Hartmann suitcase and the latest copy of *Choptalk*, the Braves monthly publication.

"She took a tumble out on the front walk."

Liza lifted her head. "Uncle Fred, are you all right? Beckett, put me down."

He lowered her to the floor, and she held on to his arm until she was certain she was steady on her feet. Poor Uncle Fred, he looked so worried. They were both drenched, rainwater trickling off their hair.

It was Beckett, eyeing the suitcase, who asked, "Mr. Grant, what gives?"

Eight

"Lady on the TV said they had this hurricane shelter set up at Bay View. Thought I'd go visit for a spell."

Beckett looked at Liza. She shrugged. She was holding her hands up in front of her chest, as if she'd just finished scrubbing for surgery.

"Liza?" It was her call to make. Actually, it was Uncle Fred's call, and evidently he'd already made it. Beckett preferred to trust Liza's judgment. Her uncle showed every sign of being fairly sharp, but then his aunt Kate had been sharp, too, right up until she'd gone shopping one day and forgotten to come home. Forgotten where she lived. Someone who knew the family had seen her sitting on a bench outside a hardware store and noticed she was still there a couple of hours later. He'd called Uncle Lance, who had been frantically searching for her at the shopping mall.

"I think that sounds like fun, Uncle Fred. Do you have everything you need? What about your glasses? Did you think to pack your medicine?"

"Yep. Got ever'thing I need. You want to drive me over there, son? She don't much like to drive at night." He nodded at Liza, who was obviously trying hard to disguise the increasing pain she was feeling.

It had been a long time since Beckett had suffered a skinned knee, but he hadn't forgotten how it stung, aside from the bruised aspect. Once the burning stage ended, she was going to be hobbling around, trying not to break the scabs and start it to bleeding all over again.

"I'll drive, Mr. Grant. Liza, you go start cleaning up your wounds. Better yet, just sit down and close your eyes for a few minutes and let me do it when I get back."

"Oh, don't fuss so, for heaven's sake. I told you I'm all right."

But as soon as they'd left, Liza drew in a deep, shuddering breath, far more shaken than a simple tumble would ordinarily cause. It was more than the fall, she realized as she watched Beckett escort her uncle out to the car, holding his arm and skirting wide of the front walk. It was...everything. The expectations she hadn't dared admit when she'd set out earlier tonight. The way the man had managed to impress her so that she couldn't stop thinking about him, even when he was hundreds of miles away. Especially then. It was almost as if he exerted some sort of gravitational pull on her.

My God, how could it have happened so quickly? It felt remarkably like her first teenage crush, only magnified a hundred times.

She hooked the screen, remembered to unhook it in case Beckett came back, and turned toward her bedroom. He had family in Charleston. Bay View was only a few miles up the road, but what if he decided to keep on going, since he was headed in that direction?

He said he was coming back, didn't he?

Lifting her sodden skirt—it was muddy, but not torn as far as she could tell—she winced at the sight of her filthy, bleeding knees. She didn't even want to think about how they were going to feel while she was scrubbing away the mud and grit. Good thing the medical frontier had advanced beyond those old antiseptics that burned like fire. She had a tube of something or other in the medicine cabinet that would soothe and disinfect.

No Band-Aids large enough, though. She'd just have to bind her knees up in gauze and learn how to walk stiff legged.

"You klutz, you stupid klutz," she muttered as she hobbled into the bathroom. Using only her fingertips, she unbuttoned the waistband of her skirt and let it fall to the floor, not even attempting to tackle her top. If it weren't soaking wet she might even sleep in it rather than use her stinging hands to change into something else. The sooner she got them cleaned and smeared with something to keep the air from touching them, the sooner they'd stop hurting.

Clumsy. Stupid. Embarrassing. She thought all that and more as she braced herself and turned on a stream of warm water. Turning an ankle might not have been so bad—even fainting. *Swooning,* as it had been called back in the days when it had been considered romantic.

There was nothing the least bit romantic about taking a damned pratfall. Even knowing she would never see him again once this debt thing was settled, she had really, really wanted to make a good last impression. Her romantic side, small and withered though it was, would have liked to think that somewhere in the world, an attractive man might occasionally remember her and wonder what would have happened if they'd met under different circumstances.

He'll remember you now, all right, she told herself, picturing the way she must have looked from his perspective. Biting her lips against the fiery pain, she thrust her hands under the water and winced as pain zinged all the way up to her armpits. Then she reached for her washcloth and soap.

Even though she tried to ignore the pain and do what had to be done, the process took longer than it should have—the cleansing, medicating and bandaging. The heels of her hands were the biggest problem. Even though they weren't quite as damaged as her knees, it made using her hands difficult. She applied the last of the gauze to her knees, then sat on the edge of the claw-footed bathtub wondering whether to put on a pair of gloves—if she could even find a pair of gloves—or risk getting her hands infected. Not to mention smearing antiseptic ointment on everything she touched.

"Well, crud," she said, fighting tears.

And then she heard the car pull up in front of the house. Had she left the door hooked or unhooked? She couldn't remember. Everything had been so confused at that point. Uncle Fred and her suitcase; the hurricane; Beckett carrying her in his arms as if she were Sleeping Beauty instead of the world's greatest klutz.

Being holed up during a storm might have been romantic under other circumstances, but not when she looked like an accident victim.

"Come in if you're coming," she yelled over the wail of the wind. The rain was beginning to blow through the screen door. She was embarassed and hurting too much to be polite.

"I'm shoving the ladder under the house for now, okay?" came the voice from the dark. The yellow porch light didn't carry far enough to see more than a shadowy figure struggling to lower the ladder without being blown over.

"Whatever," she muttered. The thought of climbing a ladder made her flinch.

A moment later he burst inside, flinging rain from his face and hair, and slammed the door behind him. "Whew! It's getting wild out there," he said, grinning as if he relished the challenge. It occurred to her that he would probably be right at home on the deck of a ship, pitching and rolling in mountainous seas. "Are you all right?" he asked. "Have you taken care of your…"

His voice trailed off as he looked down at her bandaged knees, reminding her of what she must look like in her ruined blouse, with wet hair hanging in ropes around her shoulders and her skinny, wounded legs hanging out.

Some women—the pretty, petite ones—could play the helpless heroine for all it was worth. Not Liza. She came off as a hapless clown. Okay, so she had gone overboard with the gauze. At least her knees were well padded. "Crud," she said again. Couldn't even do profanity with any style.

"Jeez, sweetheart, are they that bad? I wouldn't have left if—"

"They're skinned, all right?" she snapped. Sympathy was the very last thing she needed. She was feeling sorry enough for herself without his piling it on. And, dammit, she hurt more thinking about his walking out of her life than she did thinking about her increasingly painful injuries. Skinned knees healed in a week's time. Bruised hearts took longer. Broken hearts, she refused even to consider. She hadn't known him long enough for him to break her blasted heart.

Bracing herself, Liza took command of the situation. She might make a lousy tragic heroine, but she could play the role of gracious hostess to the hilt. She'd had plenty of practice back in the bad old days. "Come in, don't worry about tracking up the floor.

Let me get you a towel and I'll see about heating us some soup. Do you think Uncle Fred will be all right there? What if he decides he wants to come home in the middle of the night? Was it very crowded? Do you think he's acting…well, rationally? Maybe I should have insisted he stay here where I could keep an eye on him. I mean—"

So much for gracious hostess. She was falling apart, pure and simple.

Beckett took her arm and steered her toward the living room. "Go sit down, let me heat us some soup."

Liza let him take charge. Just for the moment, she told herself. Just until she could stop babbling and pull herself together. She was shivering, and it certainly wasn't cold. She was simply…

Well, hurting, for one thing. And hungry. And for no reason at all she suddenly felt like crying. "Did you bring in the groceries?"

Beckett smacked himself on the forehead. "I don't know about the meat and bread, but the milk and canned goods will probably be all right." He'd had a bag in each arm when he'd seen her stumble. No telling what had happened to them—he hadn't noticed them when he'd walked the old man out to the car. But then, he'd been holding on to his arm, watching both their steps.

On the way back, he'd been too anxious about Liza, worried that she was more shaken up than she'd let on. For a man who was generally considered pretty cool under pressure, he was flat-out losing it.

Nor did he care to define the meaning of the word *it*.

While Beckett found a basket and went out to retrieve the sodden groceries, Liza made her way from room to room, making certain all the windows were closed as tightly as possible. They were rattling in their frames, so she didn't hold out much hope, especially as the rain seemed to be coming from all directions.

Which meant the house would be stifling. If the power went off, she wouldn't even have her electric fan for comfort.

Probably wouldn't sleep, anyway.

Beckett insisted on cooking supper. He said something more substantial than soup was called for. While the ground-beef patties, seasoned with soy sauce, were cooking, he gathered up all her empty containers and filled them with water. "Just in case," he said. "If you've got a barrel or an empty garbage container, I'll set it under the eaves to collect flushing water."

"The gutter's down on the front."

"Right. Okay, the back then. If it keeps on at this rate, we won't even need a downspout."

While he was seeing to all that, Liza turned the burgers, then searched the drawers for spare batteries. She remembered reading somewhere that water and spare batteries were important.

"I don't suppose you have a weather radio," he said, coming in through the back door. She stared at him. With his clothes clinging like a second skin to a body that was muscular and whipcord lean, it took a minute for the words to register.

"A weather what?"

"Radio. You know, a dedicated NOAA receiver." He pronounced it "Noah."

She said, "You're not talking about Noah and the ark. No, even I know better than that."

She was standing by the stove. He came and removed the spatula from her fingers, skillfully turned the meat and replaced the lid. "What do you mean, even you?"

Shrugging, she moved away to stare out the window. "Nothing. It was a figure of speech, that's all."

He looked as if he didn't believe her, but then, that was his problem, not hers. She knew her shortcomings as well as she knew her longcomings. And while the former might have once outweighed the latter, she'd come a long way in the past two years. What was it they said in academic circles? Publish or perish?

In her case it had been survive or perish. She had chosen to survive.

The burgers were surprisingly tasty, even without buns. James would have been horrified—he'd fancied himself something of a gourmet. At least, he subscribed to the magazine and left it lying around along with her copies of *Art and Antiques* to create a certain impression on the people he invited to their home. If he'd ever done more than glance at either publication, she'd be very much surprised.

Beckett cut her meat for her, shushing her when she'd protested.

"I suggest you get ready for bed while I clean up the kitchen. If you don't mind, I'll commandeer your sofa again."

"Have you called home yet?" He's not leaving tonight, she thought gleefully.

"Checked in before I left Bay View. Nice place, by the way. Have you ever seen it?"

"A few times, when I drove Uncle Fred to visit some of his friends. It's a beautiful location." She'd heard it had been endowed by an elderly philanthropist. Certainly none of Uncle Fred's friends would have been able to afford it otherwise. "How are things in Charleston?"

"Wet. Mama's roses caught hell again, but other than that, everything came through just fine. My cousin Carson says hello, by the way. He was there when I called."

"Well. I know you're relieved." She was standing awkwardly beside the kitchen door, painfully aware of what she must look like. Neither of them had changed into dry clothes. It was extremely hot in the house, particularly in the kitchen.

"Uh…Liza? Do you need any help? I mean, with your hands and all…?"

But supper was over now. They could either sit in the living room watching TV as long as they had power, or go to bed and lie awake staring into the stifling darkness while the storm wore itself out and passed on up the coast. As tired as she was, she knew she wouldn't sleep.

And it wasn't the thought of the storm that would keep her awake. It was the thought of the man just a few feet away.

Beckett of the chiseled bronze features, the pewter hair and the quicksilver eyes. Becket of the square-palmed, long-fingered hands, the comforting shoulders and the hard, flat abdomen.

She quickly lifted her eyes to the ceiling. "The attic. I need to set out buckets under the leaks," she blurted.

"Stay here, I'll do it. Where do you keep your buckets?"

The buckets were all filling with rainwater, so she supplied pots and plastic wastebaskets, then waited at the foot of the stairs while Beckett set them under any drips he found in the cramped attic space. The thought of climbing the stairs was too painful to contemplate.

She tried to imagine how she'd be feeling if she'd been seriously injured—broken a leg or worse. She was one of those fortunate individuals who had never been seriously ill. Good thing, considering she'd turned out to be such a wimp.

"That's done." He descended, grinning and brushing his hands together. "Now, what do you say we switch on the fans and try to get some sleep?"

"You know where the linens are. You'll pardon me if I don't offer to make up the couch for you? I've just learned that I despise physical pain."

They were standing too close in the narrow stair landing. She could smell his shaving cream—he had obviously showered and shaved just before picking her up to go out for dinner. All that seemed aeons ago, but only a few hours had passed.

"Remind me never to accept a dinner date with you again," she said dryly.

"Remind me never to ask you for another date." He smiled, but the intensity of his look lingered after the smile had faded. She averted her face, her pulse suddenly kicking into overdrive.

Instead of moving away, he continued to stand in the attic doorway. "Liza?"

Just that. He said her name, and that was all it took. When he opened his arms, she moved into them as if he were a magnet and she a splinter of steel. No words were needed. Lifting her, he carried her to the bedroom door, then had to back up and reposition himself to maneuver her through the opening without bumping her legs.

"It never happens this way in the movies."

"Wider doorways," he said gravely. She snickered and he grinned, but the tension remained unabated. Carefully he lowered her to the bed. She held her breath. If he left her now, she didn't know what she would do. Beg him to stay? Swear at him? She was no better at begging than she was at cursing.

He reached for the tail of her shirt, eased it carefully over her head and draped it over the foot of the bed. "Liza? Are you all right with this?"

Was she all right with what? Letting him undress

her? That depended on whether it was an act of pity or an act of seduction.

Mutely she nodded. His eyes narrowed, and then he asked, "Where are your scissors?"

"My scissors," she repeated. She was sitting here naked except for a skimpy bra, matching panties and three miles of gauze, and he wanted a pair of *scissors?*

To cut off what?

"Kitchen shears in the third drawer down beside the sink, nail scissors in the medicine cabinet. Take your pick."

He left, returning a moment later with the nail scissors and a roll of adhesive tape. "Might as well get you more comfortable before we…"

Before we *what?* she wanted to scream at him.

Gently but methodically, he removed several yards of gauze from her knee, retaped the rest and used the excess to bandage her hands, wincing at the sight of her raw flesh. Finally, setting the scissors and tape roll on the dresser, he said, "There now, that's better."

She started to make a crack about playing doctor, but thought better of it. Obviously, she'd misread the signs.

But then he reached for his belt. While she watched, hardly daring to breathe, he shed his khakis and tossed them across a chair.

Neat, but not overly so, she couldn't help but notice. James would have spent minutes brushing off imaginary specks and wrinkles, draped his trousers carefully over the mahogany clothes rack and then spent even more time taking care of his shirt and tie. It was no wonder their sex life had never been terrific. By the time he was ready to come to her bed, she'd usually been half-asleep.

He was tanned all over, from his feet upward. And upward led past some breathtaking scenery. In a pair of navy boxers, he was visibly aroused. Aroused and perfectly in control. That was somehow even more exciting than being aroused and out of control.

They were adults, Liza reminded herself. He was probably better at this than she was—he had to be more experienced. She tried to swallow, but her mouth was too dry. Other parts of her body were damp and throbbing. She felt like a nervous virgin, unsure of how to act, wanting so much to please, terrified that she wouldn't. Dressed in a designer gown, with her hair professionally done and her face carefully made up, she might have felt more confident, but stick-skinny and practically naked, with big, clumsy bandages on her hands and knees, confident was the last thing she felt.

"Liza, stop it," Beckett said quietly. "If you don't want to do this, then just say so. I might not be able to walk upright for a while, but I'll survive. All you have to do is tell me to leave, and I'll spend the rest of the night on your potatoes."

She blinked. "On my *what?*"

All innocence, he said, "Don't you store your excess stock of potatoes in your sofa cushions? I could've sworn…"

She sputtered, then burst out laughing. Before she could recover, he came down beside her, kissing his way up her throat while he skillfully unhooked her bra and peeled it off.

And then his mouth found hers and all rational thought fled. Her breasts, modest at best, swelled to his touch, her nipples rising to his kisses. Her thighs first clamped together, then fell apart and she forgot all about her injuries. His back felt warm and slick as she stroked it with her fingers, wishing her hands weren't swathed in gauze so that she could stroke him with her palms. She was still smiling when he removed her panties, carefully easing them over her knees. She felt an urge to giggle. In her wildest imagination she could never have come up with a seduction scene like this, but, oh, it was working. She lay there, helpless to take a much more active part, and relished every single sensation as he brought her to the brink, allowed her to drift back, then swept her up again. First with his hands, then with his mouth, he took her places she had never before been.

By the time he moved over her, she was frantic with need. "Please, please," she gasped.

Swearing softly, he swung himself up and reached for his pants. "God, I hope it's still here." His wallet hit the floor. Rolling onto her side she curled around him as he ripped open the foil packet. Moments later he was back, positioning himself over her again, and she reached for him, never mind her bandaged hands.

It was everything she had ever imagined and more. Within minutes she climaxed not once, but twice.

Later, when she could think rationally again, she thought of the times she had accused the authors of all those romances she'd read of exaggerating. The truth was, they hadn't done it justice.

Sometime later Liza awoke, sore but relieved to find him still there beside her, curved around her back, his arm around her waist. She had never been prone to messy emotions, but suddenly her eyes were burning and her throat had that thick feeling that meant tears weren't far away.

She knew what she wanted. She wanted it to go on this way forever.

It wasn't going to happen. He'd be leaving today; she'd known that all along. She could take his money or not. She'd done nothing to earn it, yet if she refused, he might construe it as a means of holding on to him. There was nothing she'd like better than to hold on to him, but not that way.

Meanwhile, she reminded herself, there were buckets to empty in the attic, and windowsills to mop up. Hard, blowing rains always leaked through. Maybe she could take the money and use it to buy storm windows...although the whole house was so far off square, she doubted if she'd be able to find any to fit.

What on earth was she doing, lying here beside the man who had sent her over the moon again and again—thinking about *storm windows*?

There's no hope for you, Lizzy, none at all, she jeered silently. Here she'd been priding herself on the progress she'd made since her whole world had fallen apart, and now this. Now she'd gone and fallen in love with a—with a pirate chaser, of all things.

Oh, God, I don't believe this. She groaned—silently, she hoped.

"In pain, are we?" said a sleepy voice from beside her.

"No, we are not in pain," she snapped. "At least I'm not, I don't know about you."

He lay there, staring up at the ceiling, a slant of sun highlighting his bristles on his jaw. Evidently, he was one of those men who needed to shave twice. "Not a morning person, hmm?"

She was so a morning person, but it seemed childish to insist. Sitting up, she pulled the sheet over her bare breasts and braced herself to swing her legs out of bed.

"Easy," he cautioned, reading her intentions. "I wouldn't be surprised if you don't have a few bruises to show for your fall last night."

Which one? When it came to which fall would hurt the longest, there was no contest. "At least there's no point in hurrying out to the stand this morning. Why don't you shower and get dressed, and I'll make you some breakfast before you leave."

He was quiet for so long, she stole a look at him. Surely that wasn't anger she saw on his face? Lips clamped tight; jaw squared; those coal-black eyebrows that contrasted so dramatically with his hair practically glowering at her. "Beckett? Are you all right?"

"You're dead set on getting rid of me, aren't

you?'' he asked, his voice silky enough to put her on guard.

"I only offered—''

"I know what you offered, dammit.''

All right, Liza, time to take charge. She might not be used to waking up with a man who was practically a stranger in her bed, but it was no more disconcerting than what had happened to her back in Dallas. She had taken charge then; she could do it again. The storm was obviously over. Her one-night stand had been terrific. But it was just that: a once-in-a-lifetime thing. He hadn't offered more and she was too proud to beg.

She said, "Give me a minute in the bathroom first, okay?" Gritting her teeth, she eased out of bed, took a deep breath and stood, waiting for the pain to ease. Then she hobbled, stiff legged, toward the door.

"Hurts, huh?''

"I'll live.''

"Trouble with injuries like that, you can't sew 'em up, you just have to grow new skin.''

"If your shirt's still wet, you might want to hang it on the line. It should be dry by the time you're through with breakfast.''

He was watching her, dammit. She could feel his eyes on her backside as she hobbled to the door, clutching her damp shirt in front of her. *Idiot! It's not your pitiful boobs he's staring at, it's your scrawny rump!*

The mere thought of having to bend her knees to step into a pair of panties made her cringe. She'd simply have to find something to wear that would cover her decently without much underneath.

"You won't be able to drive for a while, you know," he said so close behind her she jumped. She hadn't heard him, but then, breathing through clenched teeth was a rather noisy process.

"I'll manage."

"Don't be a damned martyr, Eliza. Would it kill you to ask for help?"

Nine

Beckett took a moment to gather his thoughts after clipping his cell phone onto his belt. His last call to Carson had relieved him on several points. PawPaw was holding his own and might even be allowed to go home in another week or so if a private nurse could be found.

And one could, of course. When it came to seeing to the welfare of her family, Rebecca Beckett was more than a match for any five-star general.

The storm had passed by offshore, doing little more than surface damage. "Your end of the coast probably took more of a beating than ours," Carson had said early this morning. "How'd you and your fair lady fare?"

"Fair. A few minor scrapes, a few leaks, a few

branches down. Nothing too serious.'' He wasn't about to elaborate, not until he'd analyzed the data and decided on a course of action.

As to how Beckett himself had fared, that might be another story. He'd set himself up for what had happened, coming back again and again on a mission that had waited a hundred years and could easily wait another hundred.

Except for PawPaw. He couldn't go back and report failure; neither could he lie about it. Which meant he was stuck here until they reached an agreement regarding the money. If nothing else, he could set up an account in a local bank in her name. It would help to know where she banked, but it wasn't the sort of question a man could easily work into a conversation. From the looks of things, she probably didn't have much left to deposit after the usual monthly outlays.

Despite the fact that his family had always had money, Beckett was no snob. At least, he didn't think he was. Still, it struck him as all wrong for a woman like Liza Chandler to be eking out a living selling fruits and vegetables. She was no Eliza Doolittle. The woman had style. She had class. She had intelligence and integrity.

Not to mention sex appeal that was all the more potent because it was so understated. If she'd done anything to attract his attention, he might have been able to resist, but she hadn't. Just the opposite, if anything.

Granted, he had a weakness for needy women.

Maybe it was genetic; maybe it was an acquired trait—he didn't know. He did know he had trouble refusing any woman who'd ever asked for his help.

Liza Chandler was needy as hell, only she refused to admit it, much less accept his help. What woman in her right mind, with a roof that was about to fall in, would turn down ten grand, no strings attached?

"I'm out of the bathroom if you want to shave before you go. Didn't you mention something about seeing someone up in Virginia?"

Virginia. Newport News. McKee Shipping. He'd forgotten all about it. "I'm in no hurry," he called back. He'd never even gotten around to making an appointment. "I'll bring down the buckets from the attic."

"Just empty them out the window, it's a lot easier than trying to bring them down the stairs."

She was stalking around the house like a giraffe, mopping up windowsills and throwing open windows. Barefoot, with her hair in an off-center ponytail, she was wearing something that looked as if it was made to go over a tent pole. And all he could think of was taking her back to bed, making love to her until they both collapsed.

Great. Just bloody, blasted great. He was damned if he stayed and damned if he left. He had a feeling that Dublin wouldn't be far enough to cut him loose from her spell.

Worse, he didn't know if he even wanted to be cut loose.

Beckett knew from experience that he was bad

news to any woman looking for more than a brief fling. Maybe it was a conditioned reaction, a defense against his weakness for needy females, but it didn't change the facts. He'd been running from commitment far too long.

Not that Liza was looking for anything long-term. Not from him, at any rate. Over the years he'd gotten pretty good at reading the signals, and the only signals he'd picked up from her were confusing, to say the least. On the other hand he knew damn well that she was as conscious as he was of the physical awareness that had sprung up so unexpectedly between them. Uneasy, awkward and inappropriate as it was, recent circumstances had only served to heighten that awareness.

Once they'd ended up in bed, he'd put her awkwardness down to her injuries. Now he was beginning to wonder if there hadn't been something else behind it. The woman had been married for what, eleven years? Had the jerk been a eunuch as well as a crook?

From a few things Fred Grant had said that first night, Beckett had learned that she hadn't gone out on a single date in all the time she'd been living here. Which probably meant she was lonely. And lonely women were vulnerable. Lonely women had been known to latch on to the first reasonably healthy, solvent and available man who showed an interest in them.

Beckett qualified on all counts. Add to that the spice of the sexual attraction that had unexpectedly sprung up and it was trouble waiting to happen. A smart man would have been gone before things got out of hand.

Trouble was, he had never claimed to be smart where women were concerned. Wary, was more like it. His first experience had set the stage for that. At twenty-two he'd thought he knew it all. He'd thought that because his family was prone to long, happy marriages, it would happen for him whenever he was ready.

And he'd been ready. Ripe for the picking. Fresh out of college with family money behind him, he'd been ready to launch a career. It hadn't taken much to convince him he needed a wife at his side. Someone to help him keep his eye on the ball.

What a pathetic jerk he'd been. Shows you what comes of having a happy childhood, he thought now with no real bitterness. You grow up with unrealistically high expectations, and then one day, whammo! You wake up in the real world. There ought to be a vaccination.

Even now he could remember the scene. Both families already seated in a church that was overflowing with guests, the whole place reeking of flowers and carpet cleaner. The organist giving it her all while he stood there wondering if his collar had somehow shrunk a full size since he'd put it on less than an hour earlier.

The organist paused, waiting for a signal to launch into the pièce de résistance, when a kid about five or six years old darted in through a side door, slipped him a note and ducked out again.

Puzzled, Beckett had read the few lines in growing disbelief. He'd stood there for what seemed like an eternity, and then he'd looked up at all the curious faces: friends, family—people he'd known all his life—and told them calmly that the wedding was off.

Pam's family had blamed Beckett; his family had blamed Pam. Never mind that she and her new conquest, a middle-aged drugstore mogul, had already left for Bermuda. He never did know what happened to all the postfestivities food. He'd ripped the tin cans and ribbons off the back of his car and headed out of town with no particular destination in mind. Eventually he'd wound up at his best man's cottage on Kiawah Island, where he'd gotten royally soused on vintage champagne and been sick as a dog for days afterward.

Since then, the word *commitment* hadn't been in his vocabulary. He'd enjoyed a number of brief, mutually satisfying relationships, but he wasn't about to do to any woman what Pam had done to him. In retrospect, he figured she'd done him a big favor.

Now it was time to pass on the favor by moving out before any real damage was done. He both liked and respected Liza Chandler for the way she'd pulled herself through what had to have been a grueling experience. The last thing she needed, he told himself, was to get involved with a guy who would take all she had to offer and leave her to deal with his absence.

No way. The biggest favor he could offer her was

to get out before things got too complicated. Now that the storm had passed he would simply thank her and—

Wrong. She might take his thanks the wrong way.

Okay, so he wouldn't thank her, he'd just explain why he had to leave and—

Oh, hell. Why not just hand her the money and go?

But first he had chores to do. She would have enough to handle without having to climb those stairs half a dozen times. Anything that required bending those knees was going to be a problem for the next several days. Which meant he'd have to offer to bring the old guy back home.

He'd better check out the stand, too, else she'd be out there struggling with that section of tin roof. It would never occur to her to hire someone to do the work. Dammit, why couldn't she take the money and build something decent, as long as she insisted on staying here?

And she'd stay, of course, as long as the old guy needed her. That was something else about her he liked. Loyalty.

By the time he came downstairs with both hands full of empty containers, she was standing on the back porch, gazing out over the flattened cornfield beyond. He turned over the buckets on the edge of the porch and came to stand beside her.

"Did you ever see such a gorgeous sky?" she murmured.

"Yeah. Matter of fact, you see those colors a lot in the tropics. Don't ask me why."

She was holding her hands up in postscrub position

again, palms inward. The bandages were damp and filthy. He couldn't see her knees for the denim tent that touched her shoulders, skimmed her breasts and flowed around her like a circus tent. "Want me to look at your hands before I go?"

"No point in it," she said airily. "I'm all out of gauze. I'll get some more while I'm out."

"Out? You're planning on driving in that condition?"

The look she shot him could be described as haughty, but he recognized defensiveness when he saw it.

Damn.

"Uncle Fred's probably dying to get home by now. I thought I'd wait until the grocery store has had time to restock and stop by on the way home."

"Why don't I go for you?" Beckett heard himself asking, just as if he hadn't planned on making his excuses, thanking her for her hospitality and hitting the road before he got in any deeper.

She hesitated, then said, "Thanks, Beckett, I'd appreciate it. You'd better get several rolls of gauze and some more of that ointment while you're out, too, if you don't mind. I'll reimburse you for everything when you get back."

He wouldn't argue with her now. Instead, he would strike a bargain. He would take her money if she'd take his. "Sure. Make a list."

"But pick up Uncle Fred before you go shopping, will you? He likes to sit in the parking lot and watch people come and go."

"As good as holding a reception." He'd seen the way the old guy held court out at the roadside stand.

By the clear light of morning, she looked even paler than usual, with shadows around her eyes and a faint pink rash on her throat where his beard had rubbed against her. Her hair was still shower damp, with red-gold strands curling on the surface. Remembering the warm weight of it in his hands only a few hours ago gave rise to a reaction that was both untimely and inappropriate. Not to mention downright embarrassing.

"I'll go make that list," she said, sidling past him to escape inside the house.

Thank God one of them still retained a few grains of common sense.

He gave her enough time to make a list before he followed her inside. She was in the kitchen, awkwardly digging a spoon into a jar of peanut butter. Neither of them had taken time for breakfast. Of all crazy things, it was when he saw the guilty look on her face that Beckett knew he was fighting a losing battle.

"You know what they say about emergencies," she said with that too quick, too bright smile again. "You need more fuel. The last time I got caught eating peanut butter from a jar, I was twelve years old."

It wasn't fuel he needed, it was enhanced powers of resistance. Crossing to the silverware drawer, he took out a tablespoon, then held out his hand.

By the time the red pickup pulled into the driveway, the jar was half-empty, Liza was holding up her skirt and frowning at the frayed bandages on her knees, and Beckett had surrendered to the inevitable: no way was he going anywhere, not until they had dealt with all the unfinished business between them. And this time he wasn't thinking about the damned money, either.

The doorbell rang.

Liza dropped her skirts, mumbled, "'Scuse me," and stalked off to answer the door. Beckett figured either a neighbor or someone from Bay View must have brought the old guy home.

"Patty Ann!" He heard her exclaim from the front hallway. "What on earth...! Come inside. We're in sort of a mess right now on account of the storm— did you know about the storm? Well I guess you did, with all the rain and wind we had last night."

This was obviously not the time to settle things between them. Waiting until she herded her company into the living room, he'd intended to poke his head through the doorway and tell her he was leaving and would be back in a couple of hours. It would take that long to get the old guy's things together, get him out to the car and then stop for the groceries and first aid supplies.

Patty Ann—whoever she was—was not alone. Seated beside her on the potato-stuffed sofa was a big guy with rookie cop written all over him. Brush cut, small eyes busy taking inventory of the shabby old room.

Something triggered a silent alarm. Not danger,

just…trouble. Stepping inside the room, he said, "Morning, folks. You headed back to the beach?"

"Oh, Beckett, this is Patty Ann Garrett. She used to work for me back in Dallas, and this is—Mr. Camshaw?"

Big guy. Wrestler's torso, thick neck, face like a high-school heartthrob. Beckett stepped inside the room and extended his hand, first to the woman, a pocket Venus with freckles and a minor overbite— then to the man who rose slowly to tower a couple of inches over Beckett's own six-one. Mutt and Jeff, he thought, wondering what the devil they were doing here at this particular time.

"We were, um…in the neighborhood and thought we'd stop by," Camshaw said. "Patty Ann, she's been sort of worried about you, Ms. Edwards, not knowing where you was and all."

"How *did* you know where she was?" Beckett asked, taking care not to let his growing suspicions show in his voice. For some reason these two were hedging. He knew guilt when he saw it, and it was guilt he saw in the girl's eyes. The way they darted around. The way her blue-tipped fingers kept stroking nonexistent wrinkles from her miniskirt.

It was the guy who answered. "Patty Ann, she come across this address book mixed up in some old magazines she brought home. It had this address in it, and she was pretty sure Fred Grant was a cousin or something."

"He's my great-uncle," Liza murmured. "But how

did you know…I mean, how could you possibly know…?"

Beckett read the growing doubt in Liza's face. Putting two and two together, he came up with…two. The hang-up calls and the letter she'd told him about. A blank sheet of paper with a Dallas return address.

Oh, yeah, this pair was up to something all right. But what? Could they have been mixed up in some way with Edward's business?

Camshaw's eyes were never still. He was sweating, but then the temperature was already in the high eighties. The girl looked as if she wanted to be anywhere but where she was.

Liza asked how her mother was and got a monosyllabic reply.

"She's fine. Real good." The girl squirmed. Either she needed to go to the bathroom or she had something on her mind.

Beckett turned to Camshaw. "You're in law enforcement, right?"

The girl brightened. "How did you know that?"

He shrugged. "Lucky guess." He'd been working with law enforcement types for years.

"Cammy's just a security guard now, but he's studying to be a detective. We're going to open us this agency—you tell 'em about it, Cammy." And without pausing, she rushed on to say, "We're going to call it Camshaw and Camshaw, Private Investigations at Bargain Rates, and we thought—that is…" Her enthusiasm leaked out like air from a punctured balloon.

Beckett was beginning to get a glimmer of what it was they'd thought. Make a connection to a high-profile case, wait awhile, revisit the principals, then reap the publicity. It would be tabloid stuff, at best, but when you were trying to launch yourself as a P.I., any free press was welcome.

He wondered if either of them was aware of the fine line between jumping on a perceived opportunity and taking advantage of an innocent victim.

"We appreciate your stopping by, don't we, Liza?" He moved closer to her chair and rested his hands possessively on her shoulders.

"What? Well, yes, of course. You didn't say where you were going, Patty Ann. I wish I could offer you hospitality, but as you can see, we're in a mess here. My uncle's coming home as soon as I can go get him, and—"

"That's all right," the freckled blonde said, jumping up and reaching for Camshaw's ham-size hand. "We can't stay, can we, Cammy? I just wanted to— That is, long's we were in the neighborhood..."

Yeah. Sure you were, Beckett thought, wishing he could have just five minutes alone with the guy. While he was pretty sure they were no real threat, he had no intention of heading south while they were still in the area. It wasn't as if Liza had anything of value to steal—all the same, something didn't smell right.

"At least let me offer you some refreshments before you go," Liza said. "Coffee? Iced tea? Fruit?"

Ragged bandages, baggy tent dress and all, she was

totally convincing as the gracious hostess. Real dignity, he told himself, had little to do with outward appearances.

The phone rang, and he excused himself. "Might be for me," he said quietly as he headed for the kitchen.

It wouldn't be for him. Car would've called on his cell phone. Just as he reached for the instrument, his glance fell on the peanut butter jar with two spoons in it, and he had to smile. The lady was a constant surprise, not to mention a constant delight.

"Grant residence, Beckett speaking."

Ten

"**H**ey? Speak up, I can't hear ya. Is this Liza?"

It took a while, but Beckett managed to get the message. Uncle Fred would like to stay a few more days. Could Liza please pack a few more things and bring them out to the home? Don't forget his Bible and the picture on the mantel. Oh, and a bag of those orange-flavored prunes.

Beckett stood on the porch and watched the younger couple off before passing on Fred Grant's message. Liza said nothing. She sighed, turned and leaned her face against his chest, murmuring an apology she didn't mean and he didn't need. His arms came around her, and he held her for several long moments, savoring the feel of her, the scent of shampoo and peanut butter. "You all right?"

"No. Yes. Well, of course I am." She leaned back to look up into his face. "You know, the strangest thing…I think those two were up to something and for some reason they changed their mind. I mean, I've known Patty Ann for years, and I've never seen her so…so squirmy."

Squirmy. He'd have put it another way, but yeah…that pretty well described it. "Any ideas?"

"Nope. You?"

"A few. I think it might've had something to do with what happened a couple of years ago in Dallas. The guy's trying to launch a business, right? I doubt if they'd be spending money on a cross-country jaunt if there wasn't something in it for them. You saw what they were driving."

Her smile turned into a grin. With the sunlight sparkling on her auburn hair, highlighting her creamy complexion, she was totally irresistible. "Their truck, you mean? I think it's a year younger than my car."

Liza wished the moment could never end. Wished she didn't have to think about things like flooded vegetable bins, and leaky roofs. "But you know the sweetest thing? Patty Ann asked me to show her to the bathroom, and while we were out in the hall, she offered to lend me money. She said she'd been saving up for when she and Cammy got married, but she didn't really need it now. She said I could pay her back when I got on my feet again. Did you ever hear anything so sweet? I nearly cried."

"I thought you looked a little weepy there."

"Who called? Not another hang-up call—that's only at night."

With his hands roaming over her back, easing the stiffness she'd felt ever since she got up this morning, Beckett said, "Your uncle wants to stay on a few more days. That okay with you?"

"Well, of course. You think he really wants to stay? He's not just saying that because he knows I'll have my hands full cleaning up around here?"

"I think he really wants to stay, and I'll help you clean up."

Closing her eyes, she savored the moment. If she was lucky there might be a few more such moments before he left. She intended to savor every one of then, and shed not a single tear when he drove off. In a matter of a few days, he had brought her more happiness than she'd ever expected to find. Contentment was one thing; sheer, mindless bliss was something else. Scarcer than hens' teeth, as Uncle Fred would say.

"You know what? I think they did it," she said suddenly.

"Think who did what?"

"Those calls—you know, the hang-up calls? I think it was Patty Ann, or at least her boyfriend. But why wouldn't she just call and say they were coming East, and ask if they could come for a visit? It's almost as if—oh, I don't know, I just had the strangest feeling about the whole thing."

Beckett said nothing. He leaned against the porch support, holding her loosely in his arms. She went on.

"I know, I know, it's crazy. Honestly, I've never been paranoid—well, not very. All the same, I got a funny feeling they were, um, looking for something? What on earth did they expect to find here? And then offering to lend me money."

He waited for her to work it out in her own mind. She had most of the pieces of the puzzle. "I think you're probably right. Whatever they were looking for, whatever they were up to, the girl's all right. She'll keep him in line, and I seriously doubt if they'll bother you again."

His hands continued to stroke her back slowly, caressing her nape under the heavy fall of hair, moving down to curve over her hips. When Liza leaned away to look up at him, he smiled that slow, lazy smile that never failed to curl her toes. To think she'd once thought those silvery eyes were cold.

If she'd had a grain of sense she would have run the minute he stepped out of that big green SUV. Now, here she was, in love for the second time in her life—or maybe the first time, because this felt so much deeper, so much richer than anything she'd ever felt for James.

And this time she was mature enough to know what to expect. Tears, followed by curses, followed by bitterness, she admitted with painful honesty. Followed by a few more vows of "never again."

"Beckett, could we please go back to bed?" she asked suddenly.

He was still for so long she wanted to drop through

the floor and disappear. "Liza? Are you sure you want that?"

"Oh, I can't believe I said that," she whispered, eyes shut tightly. Opening just one, she said, "I'm sure, but if you're not— I mean, if you're in a hurry to leave…"

He laughed aloud, the sound ringing out clearly in the fresh morning air. One more time, Liza told herself, just one more memory to savor in the years ahead, is that too much to ask? She would tuck it all away together in her memory book: the sound of his rich, baritone drawl, the feel of his hands, gentle on her body.

Two spoons side by side in a jar of peanut butter….

He led her inside. There was no pretense on either side; they both knew what was going to happen. Last night the tension that had been growing between them for days had reached flash point. This time would be slower, more deliberate. They were both tired; they could take time to savor the moment.

In his own way, L. J. Beckett was every bit as much a thief as her late husband had been. He'd stolen her heart without even trying. Now that the deed was done, she might as well enjoy it while it lasted.

Thus spoke the new Liza Chandler. James had been a real education.

In the sunlight that slanted through the east-facing bedroom window, she could see the texture of his skin, the tiny creases that fanned out from his clear gray eyes, the crisp texture of his hair. Before he could inventory all her flaws, she reached up and pressed her mouth to his. He certainly wanted her—wanted sex, at least. That much was dramatically evident.

Coals of banked desire began to glow. Tiny flames began licking in the pit of her belly. She savored the now familiar taste of him, the soft tug of his teeth on her lower lip that opened her to a deeper invasion. She was lost. Light-years beyond the reach of reason. His tongue skillfully engaged hers in a game of seduction, and she gloried in every nibble, every thrust. Any remaining defenses she'd possessed had gone down without a whimper. This was her choice. She would take the lead and live with the consequences.

His hands tangled in the fabric of her denim float as he lifted it over her head. She hadn't bothered with a bra. Stepping into underpants had been painful enough without struggling to fasten a hook behind her back. She didn't know which was worse—bandaged hands or stiff knees, but if she broke loose every scrap of gauze and adhesive tape, she was not going to let herself be handicapped. This time she intended to do more than let it happen.

For long moments after he eased her clothes off, he simply held her. She loved being held. Until Beckett had come along, it had been years since anyone had held her this way. Since anyone had held her at all. She had never even missed it, never given it a thought, until this man had walked into her life.

Beckett was here, and he was nothing at all like James. Instead he was warm and caring, strong and honorable. She couldn't look at him without wanting to touch him, and it occurred to her that she had never felt that way about James, not even in the beginning.

A rash of goose bumps broke out as Beckett nuzzled the sensitive place at the side of her throat. Her head fell back and she whimpered. Slowly, slowly... make it last, she told herself, wanting nothing more than to drag him closer and feel him on every part of her body, inside and out.

His hands, unbelievably gentle, covered her small breasts. When his thumbs feathered the tips, making them rise like small pink acorns, she gasped, inhaling his clean, musky scent. She licked the skin of his throat with the tip of her tongue, felt him shudder and knew a small surge of power. He tasted slightly soapy, slightly salty.

Mmm, delicious. She wanted more.

And so she did it again and felt his arousal surge against her. *Yes!* She exulted, this is for me! Bandaged knees and all, it had to be more then merely physical.

Although the physical alone was almost more than she could bear.

Overflowing with love, she offered him one last chance to escape, if only to prove to herself that she could handle whatever did or did not come next. "Beckett, are you sure? I mean, this probably isn't very...ohhh, smart."

"Shh, honey, no one's checking IQs."

On an emotional razor's edge, she couldn't help it—she laughed aloud.

She stroked his chest under the knit shirt that clung

to his chest and shoulders with her padded palms, feeling like a molten puddle of liquid desire.

Beckett stripped quickly and efficiently, removing something from his hip pocket first. He kept a first-aid kit in his car. It was equipped for all emergencies. "Honey, are *you* sure? I don't want you to have any regrets...ever."

In other words, Liza interpreted, he wasn't making any promises.

She hadn't expected any. Hadn't asked for any. Quickly she stifled the last shred of doubt as to the wisdom of what she was about to do. There were times when wisdom was a highly overrated quality. She held out her arms, and he came down beside her.

Sunlight gleamed on the sharp angles of his tanned face, glinted off his white teeth. She said, "Let's not talk. I can't talk and have sex at the same time. It just doesn't work that way."

"Doesn't it? Sweetheart, you could lie there reading aloud from the yellow pages and I'd still want to jump your bones, bandages and all."

"Hand me the phone book, then," she demanded, and he laughed. Laughed and nuzzled her throat, then moved up to begin kissing his way down her body. Just before he reached her navel, he lifted his head and said, "Read on—don't let me stop you."

Ignoring his teasing words, she arched her hips, oblivious to the pain of her knees. All too quickly the tension reached flash point. One more touch and she knew she would go up in flames.

And then he made that one more touch. Liza, who

had never been particularly sexual until this man had come along, opened herself to his explorations, gasping as he closed in on her most sensitive flesh. What had happened to her? She wasn't like this. Until last night she had never felt this! Never *ever* gone off like a...like a firecracker! "Please...I can't stand it," she gasped.

It built swiftly and exploded just as suddenly. Spiraling rainbows, arching and dissolving, arching and dissolving, until she was nothing but a shimmering beam of white heat.

Beckett watched her ecstasy, feeling great pride and, oddly enough, an even greater sense of humility that he'd been the one to bring her this gift. And then his own control broke and he moved over her, and when she welcomed him, it began all over again.

He began to thrust, slowly at first, but all too soon he was racing out of control. There was only the sound of groans and whimpers. The sound of his rasping breath and her shuddering, gasping sighs, and then the world went up in flames again.

Twice within minutes, Liza marveled later, when her brain began functioning once more. Until last night that had never happened to her before. Usually, once didn't even happen. Sex had always been... pleasant. Something men and women did together that meant more to the man than it did to the woman.

Last night she'd been stunned by the magnitude of her climax. Today...

How on earth was she going to get through the rest

of her life without this man? Because she knew for a fact that sex with any other man, even if she could bring herself to the point, would wither in comparison.

Beckett didn't sleep afterward. His body was exhausted, his mind racing. Every particle of self-preservation he possessed was clamoring, urging him to get the hell out of her bed before it was too late.

Studying the woman sleeping in his arms, he was reminded all over again of the reasons why this never should have happened. He'd promised himself he wouldn't let things go this far—that he would settle the debt, help her get through the storm and leave.

Almost from the first time he'd seen her there in that crazy little stand of hers, looking like a down-on-her-luck duchess in her calico apron, he'd been stunned by his own reaction. It was that attitude of hers—part pride, part vulnerability—that had gotten under his skin. It had irritated the hell out of him the first few times he'd tried to do business with her.

What he hadn't known until she had come apart in his arms was how totally, devastatingly defenseless she really was. He didn't know much about that jerk she'd been married to, except that he was a crook. He sure as hell hadn't been much of a husband. Newly widowed, she'd evidently walked away from an up-scale address with little more than the clothes on her back, only to devote herself to taking care of an old man and his rinky-dink roadside stand.

And now, along with all else she had to deal with, she was going to start piling on guilt, because whatever she said to the contrary, Liza Chandler wasn't the kind of woman to take sex lightly. He'd been with enough of that sort to know the difference. When it came to sex, she probably knew less than today's average teenager.

A drop of water plunked down on his forehead and ran off onto the pillow. The rain had stopped hours ago, but it would probably continue to drip through the ceiling for hours, maybe days. No wonder the damn roof was rotted. The whole house was probably about to fall down.

He needed to shop for her groceries, rebandage her hands and knees, make sure Rambo and his groupie were gone for good and wouldn't be bothering her again—and then he could hit the road with a clear conscience.

It wasn't going to happen.

Lying on the petrified foam rubber mattress, listening to the soft purr of her breath beside him—feeling the heat of her bottom pressed into his groin, Beckett tried to rationalize his way out of the mess he was in. He'd been a practicing adult for the past twenty-odd years. Liza was only a few years younger than he was. She knows the score, he told himself.

Nope. He'd seen her, wanted her and seduced her. Some women took a broader view of life than others. She might consider herself experienced, but she was as green as any kid—more so because she didn't realize how vulnerable she was.

With wry humor, he wondered what the chances were of pretending he had amnesia. "What? We had sex? Never happened, honey, you must have me mixed up with some other guy.''

For a supposedly intelligent man, he had managed to pull some real blunders in his life, but this one was in a class by itself.

Easing out of bed, he located his pants and headed for the shower. It had to be going on noon, and he still had a few things to do before he could leave. Damn. You'd think he was deliberately looking for reasons to stick around.

From the bed, Liza watched him grab his clothes and make his escape. She hoped, she really did, that her last view of L. J.—Lancelot Jones Beckett— wasn't going to be him scurrying out of her bedroom, his clothes clutched in his arms and a guilty look on his face.

She got up, slipped on a T-shirt and loose jeans and stared at herself in the mirror. Yuck. Magic hadn't happened over the past hour. She was still plain old Liza, bony face, messy hair and all, only now she had a look in her eyes that shouldn't be there.

Sadness. She was finished with sadness. She'd sworn off sadness when she'd left Texas and headed east to start over again.

How many fresh starts was one woman allowed? She'd made her first one when, hungry for the close family she'd been missing ever since her mother died and her father had remarried, she had married James.

She'd made another start when she'd moved to North Carolina.

Another new start wasn't going to happen, because

Uncle Fred needed her. He'd been barely hanging on when she'd turned up on his front porch, uninvited. Somewhere he had a nephew—his wife's kin, not his own, but family was family. The nephew was a sailor of some sort, and evidently he wasn't into family relations.

Bracing one hand on the iron bedpost, Liza slid first one foot and then the other into a pair of sandals and set out to put things back in order. They still had produce out there that needed spreading out to dry. Some of it would be beyond salvation. Then there was that blasted roof....

The bathroom door opened and Beckett joined her in the kitchen. Pretending an intense interest in the list she was making, she ignored him. She'd managed to blunder through seducing the man. Trouble was, she hadn't a clue when it came to postseduction protocol. Neither of them smoked. Besides, that probably only worked in old movies.

Maybe she could come up with a smart quip, something like, Well, my, that was fun, wasn't it? Do you want a cup of coffee before you hit the road?

Yeah, that ought to do it.

He came to stand behind her chair. "Is that the list?"

"Is that what list?"

"The stuff you want from the grocery store. What about the things your uncle wanted?"

She stole a glance at him, gaining some small satisfaction from the fact that he seemed as ill at ease as she was. "This is all I can think of now. I'll get together the things to take to Bay View, but, Beckett, you really don't have to do this. I know you're eager to get back to Charleston.''

"Am I?"

Scraping her chair back, she stood and glared at him. "Stop it. Just stop it right now. I know this is awkward and embarrassing, and if you're looking for an apology, then here it is. I'm sorry, okay? Sorry I—that I—"

"I'm not," he said quietly. "Now give me the list and go round up whatever you want me to take to Fred."

Without another word she stalked off, plastic bag in hand, and filled it with the things her uncle had requested, throwing in several apples and a peach that wouldn't last another day.

"Here. Thank you very much," she snapped.

Her temper seemed to have a peculiar effect on him. He started to smile. The smile broadened to include flashing teeth and sparkling eyes.

Liza's eyes narrowed. Her jaw clenched, and then he confounded her completely by saying, "PawPaw's going to flat-out love you, honey. I'll stop somewhere on the way back and bring us a couple of barbecue sandwiches, okay?"

Eleven

To Liza it seemed as if days should have passed, but actually it had been than less two hours. The sun shouldn't be shining so brightly, she thought. The sky shouldn't be that incredible shade of blue, but it was. Glaringly bright, setting millions of diamonds to sparkling on emerald-green grass that was littered with storm debris.

It could have been worse, she told herself as she circled the house, surveying the damage—mostly minor—and making a mental list of what needed doing immediately and what could wait.

Another section of gutter had come down last night and was lying across the hood of the old Packard. More shingles blown off—no big surprise there. One of the oaks had lost a big limb, and the front yard was littered with leaves, twigs and green acorns. She would have to rake and tote, as Uncle Fred called it—but not today. Today she had other priorities.

Such as seeing Beckett off with a smile that would linger in his heart long after he'd said goodbye.

Oh, sure. "Grow up, Eliza," she muttered, hurling a short, dead branch over into the cornfield.

Her immediate concern was the stand. Everything inside the security fence would be drenched, but otherwise more or less intact. She had covered the cash register—her roadside antique—with a large plastic garbage bag. The three country hams she'd taken to the house, along with the soft goods. Water shouldn't hurt the produce as long as it dried off quickly enough.

In other words, she had her work cut out for her.

By half past noon, her stomach reminded her that she'd skipped breakfast. Peanut butter didn't count. And then she had to go and remember just why she'd skipped breakfast.

A few minutes later she found herself sitting in Uncle Fred's rocking chair, a sack of wet Mattamuskeet sweet onions on her lap, with tears overflowing her eyes.

It wasn't because of the onions, either.

"Well, damn," she growled, scrubbing at her cheeks with the now-filthy apron.

Carefully setting aside the onions a few minutes later, she climbed up onto her stool, hammer in hand, and managed to remove the last few nails anchoring the strip of tin roof. Once the place dried out thoroughly, she might replace it with a heavy tarp, but for now the fresh air was welcome.

She was carrying out the last few ears of corn and arranging them on the twisted tin to dry in the sunshine when Beckett pulled up in the graveled parking lot.

Oh, damn. She was filthy. Her hands…her apron. Her shoes were caked with mud, and her hair was, too, where it had escaped her clip and she'd raked it back again and again.

"What the hell do you think you're doing?" Beckett demanded.

"What does it look like I'm doing?" she returned, hoping there was no visible sign of her recent tears.

"That could've waited until I got back."

"Fine. I should've stayed in the front parlor sipping tea and reading the *Ladies' Home Journal*."

They were glaring at each other like a pair of feral dogs. Beckett held out a paper sack. "I brought lunch."

"I'm not hungry."

"Don't start with me, Liza, I've got a category-four headache."

That brought on a smile that was patently false. "Oh, what a pity. Take two aspirin and call me in the morning, all right?"

"And then you'll start with me?" The twinkle of a smile crept into his eyes, into his voice.

"You wish." Getting up off her knees, she winced, shook the wet grass and gravel from her apron and reached out for the paper sack he held tauntingly just out of reach. Her empty stomach reacted audibly to the tantalizing aroma of pit-cooked barbecue with a light, vinegary sauce.

Instead of handing over lunch, Beckett grabbed her hand. "What the hell have you been doing?" he growled.

"What do you think I've been doing?" She looked around at the onions, potatoes and cantaloupe, the watermelons and squash and corn, all of it spread out in the sunshine like a huge, colorful quilt. Some of it wouldn't make it—the rest would serve as hog food for the farmer who lived down the road. But whatever she could salvage would be produce she wouldn't have to restock.

Her shoulders drooped, and she sighed. "How's Uncle Fred holding up? Did he say when he wanted to come home?"

"As a matter of fact, we had a long talk about that. Let me get the groceries out of the car and we'll go inside and eat."

"What do you mean, you had a long talk about that? Is he coming home this afternoon? Because I really would like to do a lot more cleaning up before he sees the place. At his age, something like this can be upsetting."

Beckett steered her past the rumpled section of rusty tin roofing. He should have known she'd tackle it the minute he was gone. "Dammit, Liza, would it have killed you to ask for help?"

"I asked. You helped. What did you expect me to do, cry on your shoulder?"

Whatever he'd expected, he'd got more than he'd bargained for. A hell of a lot more. Trouble was, he didn't have it yet, not signed, sealed and delivered. "Let's get you cleaned up and rebandaged, then we'll eat, then we'll talk."

He was tempted to sweep her up in his arms and carry her up the front steps—whether on account of her scraped knees or his newly awakened caveman tendencies, he couldn't have said. Instead, he took her arm and steered her toward the house. It was time the lady learned to let someone take care of her. He was going to have a devilish time trying to convince her of it, though.

After putting a pot of coffee on to brew, he sat her down at the table, lifted her voluminous skirt and folded it back over her lap. "Hell of a thing to be working in," he grumbled, careful to keep the concern he was feeling from his voice. "Climbing up on stools, you could have—"

"But I didn't, all right?"

He grunted. "Okay, let's see how much damage you've managed to inflict on yourself."

It was a mark of how exhausted she was that she didn't protest. Beckett took full responsibility for some of her tiredness: he hadn't let her get a whole lot of rest lately.

The damage was mostly superficial, but just to be on the safe side, he bathed her injuries. When tears sprang to her eyes, he said, "Oh, hell." Laying aside the towel, he reached for her, toppling her forward. Holding her, he did his best to soothe away the fresh pain, drawing from dim memories of the way his mother had held and comforted him back when he was a brat in short pants, daring the devil and quite convinced he was invincible.

"I know, I know—hurts like hell, doesn't it? Let me pat it dry, and we'll put some more of that gunk on it. Seems to be doing the trick."

Liza took a deep, shuddering breath and nodded. He smeared antibiotic ointment on her knees and the heels of her hands. Digging into the sack of groceries, he produced a big box of gauze and proceeded to bind her wounds with yards of the stuff.

"I feel like a mummy," Liza said, feeling shaky all over again. Not from any great pain, other than the pain of seeing Beckett kneeling before her, and knowing this was probably the last hour she would ever spend with him. In which case, she would much rather have been wearing something filmy and romantic.

Or at the very least something clean.

Candles would have been a nice touch, too, although candles in a kitchen at high noon might be overdoing it. Still, a woman could dream, couldn't she?

"Poor Uncle Fred," she said, making a determined effort to shift her mind away from the mess she'd made of things. "At his age he shouldn't have to come home and find everything all torn up. He can't do much of anything himself, and he probably knows we can't afford to hire anyone. Although he's not real good when it comes to managing money. Maybe I can convince him—''

"Liza, about Uncle Fred.''

"Oh, I know, I know, he's a lot tougher than he looks, but all the same, I wish—''

"Liza, listen to me. Your uncle's been through a lot worse than the little blow we had last night. He might not be good at handling money, but he's handled more than most men—wars, depressions, grief.''

"I know that. I'm whining on his behalf because he won't. All the same...''

"All the same, there comes a time in a man's life when he wants to shed a few responsibilities, settle back and enjoy the things he can still enjoy, preferably with friends.''

"Didn't I just say that? That's why I want to get everything all cleaned up here. Then maybe I'll suggest he invite a few friends over for baseball and supper. Or maybe we'll drive down to Manteo and watch *The Lost Colony*. He told me he hasn't seen a performance since his wife died.''

Rising, Beckett shoved aside the first-aid materials just as the coffee gurgled its last gurgle. He took down two cups. Liza watched him, but made no effort to interfere. Good, he thought. He was going to need a docile Liza to get through what he had to tell her.

Over barbecue sandwiches, he brought up the first topic under consideration. "About Fred...Liza, you do know he has a nephew, don't you?''

She reached for a French fry. He snagged his lower lip with his teeth, trying to think how best to break the news. "Well, sure. I know his wife had—has—a nephew," she said. "I told you that, remember? I've never actually met him, but he calls to talk to Uncle Fred whenever he's in port. I think he works on one of those big container ships, I'm not sure."

"You're right. But he's thinking of retiring as soon as he can get on with his plans here."

"Here where?" She took a big bite of her barbecue sandwich, closed her eyes and sighed. "Heavenly. It's even better than Texas barbecue, and if that sounds traitorous, Texas can sue me."

"The lot next door?" Beckett indicated the east-facing window. To the west and north of the Grant house were cornfields. On the east side was a cleared lot surrounded by several hundred acres of soybeans.

"What about it?" she asked with her mouth full.

Leaning across the table, he brushed a streak of barbecue sauce from beside her mouth, then licked it from his thumb. "Yeah, well, the thing is, all that belongs to Fred's nephew."

"Fred's wife's nephew," she corrected. "I'm his only blood kin."

"Dammit, Liza, I'm trying to tell you that this place—the house, the lot next door—they belong to Solon Pugh. The nephew."

"In-law," she supplied, frowning.

"Right. The thing is, they don't belong to Fred."

She stopped chewing. Her eyes went round, narrowed, then widened again as she absorbed the full impact. "You mean this Pugh fellow—he's just letting Uncle Fred live here?"

This was going to be painful. He figured it was best to get it over with quickly and let the healing begin. "Fred's wife's folks built the house. It belonged to her, and when she died, it went to her nephew, with Fred retaining a lifetime right."

"So?" She had carefully laid her sandwich on the napkin. Her freshly bandaged hands were resting on her lap. "I don't see that that changes anything."

"It doesn't. You did."

"I don't think I want to hear this. If you don't mind, I'm going to go back out to the stand and—"

He caught her by the arm before she could leave. "You're going to have to hear it. Honey, Fred was all ready to move into Bay View with his friends when you turned up one day, needing a place to stay. Needing someone to help you get started again. Fred recognized that. His hearing might not be what it once was, but his mind is as sharp as ever. He called Pugh and told him he'd changed his mind and was going to stay on awhile longer. As he told me this morning, you needed something to latch on to to get you back on your feet, and he didn't mind helping you out."

"Helping me out?" Liza repeated, a stricken look on her face. "But I'm the one who was helping him. He couldn't have stayed here without me—without someone…"

He came around the table and knelt beside her, holding her while she sucked in great gulps of air. "I'm not going to cry, don't worry," she said. "Just give me a minute, will you?"

"All the time in the world, sugar babe. Go ahead and cry, if you need to, sweetheart."

That got her attention. Rearing back, she glared at him, her elegant, patrician features no less beautiful for the smear of grime across her forehead.

"What, I can't call you sweetheart?" he challenged.

"Sugar babe?"

"Hey, it's what the men in my family call the women—and the women call them that right back. It means 'I love you.' Don't people in Texas talk that way?"

"Not the people I knew."

He waited for her to pick up on what he'd said. It might come as something of a shock. It had shocked the hell out of him, but once he'd realized it had happened, he'd accepted it. Felt pretty damned good about it, matter of fact. No more running away. This was it—this was what he'd been running toward all these years.

Now all he had to do was convince Liza.

"You see where I'm going with this, right?"

"Uncle Fred wants to stay on at Bay View so that his nephew can move in here." She nodded slowly. "I understand."

Beckett's reputation as a negotiator had never been in question. He was among the best. But negotiating with hijackers—modern-day pirates—was one thing. Reaching a mutually satisfying agreement with a woman who was both proud and needy...that called for an altogether different set of skills.

For a guy who had commitment avoidance down to a fine art, he was digging his own grave here. Never had a grave been dug more willingly. "You heard what I said, then?"

She nodded. Her fingers, which were the only parts of her hands not swathed in gauze, walked their way up his chest and latched on to his collar. She still refused to meet his eyes.

"All of it?" he pressed.

"All of what?" She lifted her face then, and he caught a glimmer of what was going on behind those whiskey-colored eyes. Satisfaction began to glow inside him like banked coals.

Emboldened, he said, "You want the full, complete translation? *Hon* and *honey*—now those can mean either one of two things, depending on who's saying it to whom. It can mean either 'I love you,' or 'I'm content with who I am and hope you're lucky enough to be the same.' As for the rest—*sweetheart*—that's pretty self-evident."

"And *sugar babe?*" She was getting into the swing of things.

"Ah, yes…well now, that can mean a couple of things, too. There's the *sugar babe* that means, 'Wow, I'd sure like to get in your pants!' Then, there's the *sugar babe* that means, 'Me and you, hon—better or worse, thick or thin—side meat or sirloin, we stick together.'"

"I'm afraid to ask," she said, and darned if he didn't believe her. How the hell could she still have doubts? Hadn't he just told her he loved her? Maybe he'd circled around it a time or two, but then, he hadn't had any practice in the past couple of decades.

"Look, how about we pack up what Uncle Fred wants to keep, take it to him, then we come back here and pack up everything you need, and then we'll lock up and head south. You need to meet PawPaw, you need to meet all my folks, and then, if you'll still have me...."

Liza thought, *Oh, Lord, don't let me hyperventilate.* "I think I've just been proposed to. If not, you'd better set me straight real fast."

"Hey, I'm down on my bended knee, aren't I?" It was hard to tell under his deep suntan, but she could almost swear he was blushing.

"If you're waiting for me to get down on mine to accept, then you're going to have to give me more time."

"Sorry, time's up. What about we both get horizontal and continue this conversation?"

Liza had to laugh at that. So did Beckett, because they both knew there would be little conversation in the near future. "Know what? I can hardly wait to take you home to show PawPaw. If I didn't know better, I'd think he'd set this whole thing up on purpose."

* * * * *

presents

A brand-new miniseries about the Connellys of Chicago,
a wealthy, powerful American family tied by blood to the
royal family of the island kingdom of Altaria.
They're wealthy, powerful and rocked by
scandal, betrayal...and passion!

Look for a whole year of glamorous and
utterly romantic tales in 2002:

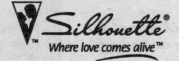

Where love comes alive™

*A powerful earthquake
ravages Southern California...*

*Thousands are trapped
beneath the rubble...*

*The men and women of
Morgan Trayhern's team
face their most heroic
mission yet...*

A brand-new series from
USA TODAY bestselling author

LINDSAY McKENNA

Don't miss these breathtaking
stories of the triumph of love!

Look for one title per month
from each Silhouette series:

August: THE HEART BENEATH
(Silhouette Special Edition #1486)

September: RIDE THE THUNDER
(Silhouette Desire #1459)

October: THE WILL TO LOVE
(Silhouette Romance #1618)

**November: PROTECTING
HIS OWN**
(Silhouette Intimate Moments #1185)

*Available at your favorite
retail outlet*

Where love comes alive™

magazine

❤ —————————————————— **quizzes**

Is he the one? What kind of lover are you? Visit the **Quizzes** area to find out!

❤ ———————————————— **recipes for romance**

Get scrumptious meal ideas with our **Recipes for Romance**.

❤ ———————————————— **romantic movies**

Peek at the **Romantic Movies** area to find Top 10 Flicks about First Love, ten Supersexy Movies, and more.

❤ ———————————————— **royal romance**

Get the latest scoop on your favorite royals in **Royal Romance**.

❤ —————————————————— **games**

Check out the **Games** pages to find a ton of interactive romantic fun!

❤ ———————————————— **romantic travel**

In need of a romantic rendezvous? Visit the **Romantic Travel** section for articles and guides.

❤ ———————————————— **lovescopes**

Are you two compatible? Click your way to the **Lovescopes** area to find out now!

Silhouette —

where love comes alive—online...

SINTMAG

July 2002
IN BLACKHAWK'S BED
#1447 by Barbara McCauley

SECRETS!

Don't miss the latest title in
Barbara McCauley's sizzling and
scandal-filled miniseries.

August 2002
BECKETT'S CINDERELLA
#1453 by Dixie Browning

BECKETT'S FORTUNE

Be sure to check out the first book in
Dixie Browning's exciting crossline
miniseries about two families, four
generations and the one debt that
binds them together!

September 2002
RIDE THE THUNDER
#1459 by Lindsay McKenna

Watch as bestselling author
Lindsay McKenna's sexy mercenaries
battle danger and fight for the hearts
of the women they love, in book two
of her compelling crossline miniseries.

MAN OF THE MONTH

Some men are made for lovin'—and you're sure to love
these three upcoming men of the month!

Available at your favorite retail outlet.

Silhouette®

Where love comes alive™

Visit Silhouette at www.eHarlequin.com   SDMOM02Q3

COMING NEXT MONTH

#1459 RIDE THE THUNDER—Lindsay McKenna
Morgan's Mercenaries: Ultimate Rescue
Lieutenant Nolan Galway didn't believe women belonged in the U.S. Marines, but then a dangerous mission brought him and former marine pilot Rhona McGregor together. Though he'd intended to ignore his beautiful copilot, Nolan soon found himself wanting to surrender to the primitive hunger she stirred in him....

#1460 THE SECRET BABY BOND—Cindy Gerard
Dynasties: The Connellys
Tara Connelly Paige was stunned when the husband she had thought dead suddenly reappeared. Michael Paige was still devastatingly handsome, and she was shaken by her desire for him—body and soul. He claimed he wanted to be a real husband to her and a father to the son he hadn't known he had. But could Tara learn to trust him again?

#1461 THE SHERIFF & THE AMNESIAC—Ryanne Corey
As soon as he'd seen her, Sheriff Tyler Cook had known Jenny Kyle was the soul mate he'd searched for all his life. Her fiery beauty enchanted him, and when an accident left her with amnesia, he brought her to his home. They soon succumbed to the attraction smoldering between them, but Tyler wondered what would happen once Jenny's memory returned....

#1462 PLAIN JANE MacALLISTER—Joan Elliott Pickart
The Baby Bet: The MacAllister Family
A trip home turned Mark Maxwell's life upside down, for he learned that Emily MacAllister, the woman he'd always loved, had secretly borne him a son. Hurt and angry, Mark nonetheless vowed to build a relationship with his son. But his efforts brought him closer to Emily, and his passionate yearning for her grew. Could they make peace and have their happily-ever-after?

#1463 EXPECTING BRAND'S BABY—Emilie Rose
Because of an inheritance clause, Toni Swenson had to have a baby. She had a one-night stand with drop-dead-gorgeous cowboy Brand Lander, who followed her home once he realized she might be carrying his child. When Brand proposed a marriage of convenience, Toni accepted. And though their marriage was supposed to be in-name-only, Brand's soul-stirring kisses soon had Toni wanting the *real* thing.

#1464 THE TYCOON'S LADY—Katherine Garbera
The Bridal Bid
When lovely Angelica Leone fell into his lap at a bachelorette auction, wealthy businessman Paul Sterling decided she would make the perfect corporate girlfriend. They settled on a business arrangement of three dates. But Angelica turned to flame in Paul's arms, and he found himself in danger—of losing his heart!

SDCNM0802